MOTHERS

MOTHERS

CLASSICS FROM THE MODERN LIBRARY

THE MODERN LIBRARY
NEW YORK

1998 Modern Library Edition

LIBRARY OF CONGRESS CATALOGING-IN-PUBLICATION DATA
Mothers: classics from the Modern Library.—1998 Modern Library ed.
p. cm.
ISBN 0-375-75153-X (pbk.)
1. Mothers—Literary collections. I. Modern Library (Firm)
PN6071.M7M684 1998
808.8'03520431—dc21 98-14562

Modern Library website address:
www.randomhouse.com/modernlibrary

Printed in the United States of America on acid-free paper

2 4 6 8 9 7 5 3 1

A Note to the Reader

"When mother reads aloud I long
For noble deeds to do—
To help the right, redress the wrong,
It seems so easy to be strong, so simple to be true,
O, thick and fast the visions crowd
When mother reads aloud."

—*from* "When Mother Reads Aloud"

Most of our early memories revolve around our mothers. In each of them, she is our protector, caregiver, educator, guide. She bandages scraped knees when we're learning to ride a bicycle, makes us chicken noodle soup and tucks in the covers when we're sick, patiently reads us our favorite stories, again and again. Motherhood can be the most difficult job in the world. The Modern Library has compiled a collection to assist in offering thanks to our mothers: recite together a few verses from Robert Louis Stevenson's *Child's Garden;* take Anne Bradstreet's "Meditations" to heart; tell your little girl about Longfellow's little girl with the little curl or your little boy about being made of "snips and snails, and puppy-dogs' tails." We hope that mothers and children alike will share in the celebration.

Contents

BIBLE EXTRACTS

The story of Mary, the Holy Mother, is found in the Gospels of Luke and Matthew. It is presented here in the Authorized (King James) Version.

The Gospel According to Saint Luke

CHAPTER 1

And in the sixth month the angel Gabriel was sent from God unto a
city of Galilee, named Nazareth,
27 To a virgin espoused to a man whose name was Joseph, of the
house of David; and the virgin's name *was* Mary.
28 And the angel came in unto her, and said, Hail, *thou that art*
highly favoured, the Lord *is* with thee: blessed *art* thou among women.
29 And when she saw *him*, she was troubled at his saying, and cast
in her mind what manner of salutation this should be.
30 And the angel said unto her, Fear not, Mary: for thou hast found
favour with God.
31 And, behold, thou shalt conceive in thy womb, and bring forth
a son, and shalt call his name Jesus.
32 He shall be great, and shall be called the Son of the Highest:
and the Lord God shall give unto him the throne of his father David:

33 And he shall reign over the house of Jacob for ever; and of his kingdom there shall be no end.

34 Then said Mary unto the angel, How shall this be, seeing I know not a man?

35 And the angel answered and said unto her, The Holy Ghost shall come upon thee, and the power of the Highest shall overshadow thee; therefore also that holy thing which shall be born of thee shall be called the Son of God.

36 And, behold, thy cousin Elisabeth, she hath also conceived a son in her old age: and this is the sixth month with her, who was called barren.

37 For with God nothing shall be impossible.

38 And Mary said, Behold the handmaid of the Lord; be it unto me according to thy word. And the angel departed from her.

The Gospel According to Saint Matthew

CHAPTER 1

Now the birth of Jesus Christ was on this wise: When as his mother
Mary was espoused to Joseph, before they came together, she was
found with child of the Holy Ghost.
19 Then Joseph her husband, being a just *man,* and not willing to
make her a publick example, was minded to put her away privily.
20 But while he thought on these things, behold, the angel of the
Lord appeared unto him in a dream, saying, Joseph, thou son of David,
fear not to take unto thee Mary thy wife: for that which is conceived
in her is of the Holy Ghost.
21 And she shall bring forth a son, and thou shalt call his name
Jesus: for he shall save his people from their sins.
22 Now all this was done, that it might be fulfilled which was spo-
ken of the Lord by the prophet, saying,
23 Behold, a virgin shall be with child, and shall bring forth a son,

and they shall call his name Emmanuel, which being interpreted is, God with us.

24 Then Joseph being raised from sleep did as the angel of the Lord had bidden him, and took unto him his wife:

25 And knew her not till she had brought forth her firstborn son: and he called his name Jesus.

FROM THE NEW ENGLAND PRIMER, CIRCA 1683

Published in various versions from 1683 to 1830, The New England Primer *was considered nearly as important as the Bible in the Puritan household. The lessons combined literacy and religion, instilling Puritan culture and moral precepts in young children while teaching them to read.* The Primer *sold an estimated five million copies over the years it was in popular use, and inspired many regional lesson books, such as* The Albany Primer *and* The Pennsylvania Primer.

The Alphabet

A

In *Adam's* Fall
We Sinned all.

B

Thy Life to Mend
This *Book* Attend.

C

The *Cat* doth play
And after slay.

D

A *Dog* will bite
A Thief at night.

E

An *Eagle's* flight
Is out of sight.

F

The Idle *Fool*
Is whipt at School.

G

As runs the *Glass*
Man's life doth pass.

H

My *Book* and *Heart*
Shall never part.

J

Job feels the Rod
Yet blesses GOD.

K

Our *KING* the good
No man of blood.

L

The *Lion* bold
The *Lamb* doth hold.

M

The *Moon* gives light
In time of night.

N

Nightengales sing
In time of Spring.

O

The *Royal Oak* it was the Tree
That sav'd His Royal Majestie.

P

Peter denies
His Lord and cries

Q

Queen Esther comes in Royal State
To Save the JEWS from dismal Fate

R

Rachel doth mourn
For her first born.

S

Samuel anoints
Whom God appoints.

T

Time cuts down all
Both great and small.

U

Uriah's beauteous Wife
Made David seek his Life.

W

Whales in the Sea
God's Voice obey.

X

Xerxes the great did die,
And so must you & I.

Y

Youth forward slips
Death soonest nips.

Z

Zacheus he
Did climb the Tree
His Lord to see.

Now the Child being entred in his Letters and Spelling, let him learn these and such like Sentences by Heart, whereby he will be both instructed in his Duty, and encouraged in his Learning.

The Dutiful Child's Promises

I Will fear GOD, and honour the KING.
I will honour my Father & Mother.
I will Obey my Superiours.
I will Submit to my Elders,
I will Love my Friends.
I will hate no Man.
I will forgive my Enemies, and pray to God for them.
I will as much as in me lies keep all God's Holy Commandments.
I will learn my Catechism.
I will keep the Lord's Day Holy.
I will Reverence God's Sanctuary,
For our GOD is a consuming Fire.

Verses

I in the Burying Place may see
  Graves shorter there than I;
From Death's Arrest no Age is free,
  Young Children too may die;
My God, may such an awful Sight,
  Awakening be to me!
Oh! that by early Grace I might
  For Death prepared be.

Again

First in the Morning when thou dost awake,
To God for his Grace thy Petition make,
Some Heavenly Petition use daily to say,
That the God of Heaven may bless thee alway.

* * *

Good Children must,
Fear God all Day, Love Christ alway,
Parents obey, In Secret Pray,
No false thing say, Mind little Play,
By no Sin stray, Make no delay, In doing Good.
Awake, arise, behold thou hast
Thy Life a Leaf, thy Breath a Blast:
At Night lye down prepar'd to have
Thy sleep, thy death, thy bed, thy grave.

POEMS

For reading aloud to or by Mother, or just for appreciating in a quiet sunny corner, we offer a selection of poems that have been familiar to us since childhood—even the cradle—ranging from "Home Sweet Home," written by playwright John Howard Payne (1791–1852) for his play Clari; or, The Maid of Milan; *to "The Children's Hour," by Henry Wadsworth Longfellow (1807–1882), the most popular poet of the nineteenth century; to "Lullaby," by Thomas Dekker (1572–1632), best known as an English dramatist and pamphlet writer.*

Presented here in full are Songs of Innocence *and* Songs of Experience, *penned by the English poet, engraver, and sometime prophet William Blake (1757–1827).*

Home, Sweet Home

John Howard Payne

'Mid pleasures and palaces though we may roam,
Be it ever so humble, there's no place like home;
A charm from the sky seems to hallow us there,
Which, seek through the world, is ne'er met with elsewhere.
Home, home, sweet, sweet home!
There's no place like home, oh, there's no place like home!

An exile from home, splendor dazzles in vain;
Oh, give me my lowly thatched cottage again!
The birds singing gayly, that came at my call—
Give me them—and the peace of mind, dearer than all!
Home, home, sweet, sweet home!
There's no place like home, oh, there's no place like home!

I gaze on the moon as I tread the drear wild,
And feel that my mother now thinks of her child,
As she looks on that moon from our own cottage door
Thro' the woodbine, whose fragrance shall cheer me no more.
Home, home, sweet, sweet home!
There's no place like home, oh, there's no place like home!

How sweet 'tis to sit 'neath a fond father's smile,
And the caress of a mother to soothe and beguile!

Let others delight 'mid new pleasure to roam,
But give me, oh, give me, the pleasures of home,
    Home, home, sweet, sweet home!
There's no place like home, oh, there's no place like home!

To thee I'll return, overburdened with care;
The heart's dearest solace will smile on me there;
No more from that cottage again will I roam;
Be it ever so humble, there's no place like home.
    Home, home, sweet, sweet home!
There's no place like home, oh, there's no place like home!

When Mother Reads Aloud

"When mother reads aloud the past
Seems real as every day;
I hear the tramp of armies vast,
I see the spears and lances cast,
I join the thrilling fray;
Brave knights and ladies fair and proud
I meet when mother reads aloud.

"When mother reads aloud, far lands
Seem very near and true;
I cross the desert's gleaming sands,
Or hunt the jungle's prowling bands,
Or sail the ocean blue;
Far heights, whose peaks the cold mists shroud,
I scale, when mother reads aloud.

"When mother reads aloud I long
For noble deeds to do—
To help the right, redress the wrong,
It seems so easy to be strong, so simple to be true,
O, thick and fast the visions crowd
When mother reads aloud."

Before the Birth of One of Her Children

Anne Bradstreet

All things within this fading world hath end,
Adversity doth still our joys attend;
No ties so strong, no friends so dear and sweet,
But with death's parting blow is sure to meet.
The sentence past is most irrevocable,
A common thing, yet oh inevitable;
How soon, my dear, death may my steps attend,
How soon't may be thy lot to lose thy friend,
We both are ignorant, yet love bids me
These farewell lines to recommend to thee,
That when that knot's untied that made us one,
I may seem thine, who in effect am none.
And if I see not half my days that's due,
What nature would, God grant to yours and you;
The many faults that well you know I have,
Let be interr'd in my oblivion's grave;
If any worth or virtue were in me,
Let that live freshly in thy memory,
And when thou feel'st no grief, as I no harms,
Yet love thy dead, who long lay in thine arms:
And when thy loss shall be repaid with gains,

Look to my little babes, my dear remains.
And if thou love thy self, or loved'st me,
These O protect from step-dame's injury.
And if chance to thine eyes shall bring this verse,
With some sad sighs honor my absent hearse;
And kiss the paper for thy love's dear sake,
Who with salt tears this last farewell did take.

In Reference to Her Children, 23 June 1659

Anne Bradstreet

I had eight birds hatcht in one nest,
Four cocks there were, and hens the rest,
I nurst them up with pain and care,
Nor cost, nor labor did I spare,
Till at the last they felt their wing,
Mounted the trees, and learn'd to sing;
Chief of the brood then took his flight,
To regions far, and left me quite.
My mournful chirps I after send,
Till he return, or I do end:
Leave not thy nest, thy dam and sire,
Fly back and sing amidst this choir.
My second bird did take her flight,
And with her mate flew out of sight;
Southward they both their course did bend,
And seasons twain they there did spend:
Till after blown by southern gales,
They norward steer'd with filled sails.
A prettier bird was no where seen,
Along the beach among the treen.
I have a third of color white,

On whom I plac'd no small delight;
Coupled with mate loving and true,
Hath also bid her dam adieu:
And where Aurora first appears,
She now hath percht to spend her years;
One to the academy flew
To chat among that learned crew:
Ambition moves still in his breast
That he might chant above the rest,
Striving for more than to do well,
That nightingales he might excel.
My fifth, whose down is yet scarce gone,
Is 'mongst the shrubs and bushes flown,
And as his wings increase in strength,
On higher boughs he'll perch at length.
My other three, still with me nest,
Until they're grown, then as the rest,
Or here or there, they'll take their flight,
As is ordain'd, so shall they light.
If birds could weep, then would my tears
Let others know what are my fears
Lest this my brood some harm should catch,
And be surpris'd for want of watch,
Whilst pecking corn, and void of care
They fall un'wares in fowler's snare:
Or whilst on trees they sit and sing,
Some untoward boy at them do fling:
Or whilst allur'd with bell and glass,
The net be spread, and caught, alas.
Or least by lime-twigs they be foil'd,
Or by some greedy hawks be spoil'd.

O would my young, ye saw my breast,
And knew what thoughts there sadly rest,
Great was my pain when I you bred,
Great was my care when I you fed,
Long did I keep you soft and warm,
And with my wings kept off all harm,
My cares are more, and fears than ever,
My throbs such now, as 'fore were never:
Alas my birds, you wisdom want,
Of perils you are ignorant,
Oft times in grass, on trees, in flight,
Sore accidents on you may light.
O to your safety have an eye,
So happy may you live and die:
Mean while my days in tunes I'll spend,
Till my weak lays with me shall end.
In shady woods I'll sit and sing,
And things that past, to mind I'll bring.
Once young and pleasant, as are you,
But former toys (no joys) adieu.
My age I will not once lament,
But sing, my time so near is spent.
And from the top bough take my flight,
Into a country beyond sight,
Where old ones instantly grow young,
And there with seraphims set song:
No seasons cold, nor storms they see,
But spring lasts to eternity.
When each of you shall in your nest
Among your young ones take your rest,
In chirping language, oft them tell,

You had a dam that lov'd you well,
That did what could be done for young,
And nurst you up till you were strong,
And 'fore she once would let you fly,
She show'd you joy and misery;
Taught what was good, and what was ill,
What would save life, and what would kill.
Thus gone, amongst you I may live,
And dead, yet speak, and counsel give:
Farewell, my birds, farewell adieu,
I happy am, if well with you.

THE CHILDREN'S HOUR

Henry Wadsworth Longfellow

Between the dark and the daylight,
    When the night is beginning to lower,
Comes a pause in the day's occupations,
    That is known as the Children's Hour.

I hear in the chamber above me
    The patter of little feet,
The sound of a door that is opened,
    And voices soft and sweet.

From my study I see in the lamplight,
    Descending the broad hall stair,
Grave Alice, and laughing Allegra,
    And Edith with golden hair.

A whisper, and then a silence:
    Yet I know by their merry eyes
They are plotting and planning together
    To take me by surprise.

A sudden rush from the stairway,
  A sudden raid from the hall!
By three doors left unguarded
  They enter my castle wall!

They climb up into my turret
  O'er the arms and back of my chair;
If I try to escape, they surround me;
  They seem to be everywhere.

They almost devour me with kisses,
  Their arms about me entwine,
Till I think of the Bishop of Bingen
  In his Mouse-Tower on the Rhine!

Do you think, O blue-eyed banditti,
  Because you have scaled the wall,
Such an old mustache as I am
  Is not a match for you all!

I have you fast in my fortress,
  And will not let you depart,
But put you down into the dungeon
  In the round-tower of my heart.

And there will I keep you forever,
  Yes, forever and a day,
Till the walls shall crumble to ruin,
  And moulder in dust away.

There Was a Little Girl

Henry Wadsworth Longfellow

There was a little girl, she had a little curl
  Right in the middle of her forehead;
And when she was good, she was very, very good,
  And when she was bad, she was horrid.

To a Child

Henry Wadsworth Longfellow

By what astrology of fear or hope
Dare I to cast thy horoscope!
Like the new moon thy life appears;
A little strip of silver light,
And widening outward into night
The shadowy disk of future years;
And yet upon its outer rim,
A luminous circle, faint and dim,
And scarcely visible to us here,
Rounds and completes the perfect sphere;
A prophecy and intimation,
A pale and feeble adumbration,
Of the great world of light, that lies
Behind all human destinies.

Lullaby

FROM *The Princess*

Alfred, Lord Tennyson

Sweet and low, sweet and low,
  Wind of the western sea,
Low, low, breathe and blow,
  Wind of the western sea!
Over the rolling waters go,
Come from the dying moon, and blow,
  Blow him again to me;
While my little one, while my pretty one, sleeps.

Sleep and rest, sleep and rest,
  Father will come to thee soon;
Rest, rest, on mother's breast,
  Father will come to thee soon;
Father will come to his babe in the nest,
Silver sails all out of the west
  Under the silver moon:
Sleep, my little one, sleep, my pretty one, sleep.

Étude Réaliste

Algernon Charles Swinburne

I

A baby's feet, like sea-shells pink,
Might tempt, should Heaven see meet,
An angel's lips to kiss, we think,
A baby's feet.

Like rose-hued sea-flowers toward the heat
They stretch and spread and wink
Their ten soft buds that part and meet.

No flower-bells that expand and shrink
Gleam half so heavenly sweet
As shine on life's untrodden brink
A baby's feet.

II

A baby's hands, like rosebuds furled,
Whence yet no leaf expands,
Ope if you touch, though close upcurled,
A baby's hands.

Then, even as warriors grip their brands
  When battle's bolt is hurled,
They close, clenched hard like tightening bands.

No rosebuds yet by dawn impearled
  Match, even in loveliest lands,
The sweetest flowers in all the world—
  A baby's hands.

III

A baby's eyes, ere speech begin,
  Ere lips learn words or sighs,
Bless all things bright enough to win
  A baby's eyes.

Love, while the sweet thing laughs and lies,
  And sleep flows out and in,
Lies perfect in them Paradise.

Their glance might cast out pain and sin,
  Their speech make dumb the wise,
By mute glad godhead felt within
  A baby's eyes.

Baby Running Barefoot

D. H. Lawrence

When the white feet of the baby beat across the grass
The little white feet nod like white flowers in a wind,
They poise and run like puffs of wind that pass
Over water where the weeds are thinned.

And the sight of their white playing in the grass
Is winsome as a robin's song, so fluttering;
Or like two butterflies that settle on a glass
Cup for a moment, soft little wing-beats uttering.

And I wish that the baby would tack across here to me
Like a wind-shadow running on a pond, so she could stand
With two little bare white feet upon my knee
And I could feel her feet in either hand

Cool as syringa buds in morning hours,
Or firm and silken as young peony flowers.

My Mother

Ann Taylor

Who fed me from her gentle breast
And hushed me in her arms to rest,
And on my cheek sweet kisses prest?
My mother.

When sleep forsook my open eye,
Who was it sung sweet lullaby
And rocked me that I should not cry?
My mother.

Who sat and watched my infant head
When sleeping in my cradle bed,
And tears of sweet affection shed?
My mother.

When pain and sickness made me cry,
Who gazed upon my heavy eye
And wept, for fear that I should die?
My mother.

Who ran to help me when I fell
And would some pretty story tell,
Or kiss the part to make it well?
My mother.

Who taught my infant lips to pray,
To love God's holy word and day,
And walk in wisdom's pleasant way?
My mother.

And can I ever cease to be
Affectionate and kind to thee
Who wast so very kind to me,—
My mother.

Oh no, the thought I cannot bear;
And if God please my life to spare
I hope I shall reward thy care,
My mother.

When thou art feeble, old and gray,
My healthy arm shall be thy stay,
And I will soothe thy pains away,
My mother.

And when I see thee hang thy head,
'Twill be my turn to watch thy bed,
And tears of sweet affection shed,—
My mother.

To an Infant

Samuel Taylor Coleridge

Ah, cease thy Tears and Sobs, my little Life!
I did but snatch away the unclasped Knife:
Some safer Toy will soon arrest thine eye
And to quick Laughter change this peevish cry!
Poor Stumbler on the rocky coast of Woe,
Tutored by Pain each source of Pain to know
Alike the foodful fruit and scorching fire
Awake thy eager grasp and young desire:
Alike the Good, the Ill offend thy sight,
And rouse the stormy Sense of shrill Affright!
Untaught, yet wise! mid all thy brief alarms
Thou closely clingest to thy Mother's arms,
Nestling thy little face in that fond breast
Whose anxious Heavings lull thee to thy rest!

Man's breathing Miniature! thou mak'st me sigh—
A Babe art thou—and such a Thing am I!
To anger rapid and as soon appeased,
For trifles mourning and by trifles pleased,
Break Friendship's Mirror with a tetchy blow,
Yet snatch what coals of fire on Pleasure's altar glow!

Characteristics of a Child Three Years Old

William Wordsworth

Loving she is, and tractable, though wild;
And Innocence hath privilege in her
To dignify arch looks and laughing eyes;
And feats of cunning; and the pretty round
Of trespasses, affected to provoke
Mock-chastisement and partnership in play.
And, as a faggot sparkles on the hearth,
Not less if unattended and alone
Than when both young and old sit gathered round
And take delight in its activity;
Even so this happy Creature of herself
Is all-sufficient; solitude to her
Is blithe society, who fills the air
With gladness and involuntary songs.
Light are her sallies as the tripping fawn's
Forth-startled from the fern where she lay couched;
Unthought-of, unexpected, as the stir
Of the soft breeze ruffling the meadow-flowers.
Or from before it chasing wantonly
The many-coloured images imprest
Upon the bosom of a placid lake.

There Was a Child Went Forth

Walt Whitman

There was a child went forth every day,
And the first object he look'd upon, that object he became,
And that object became part of him for the day or a certain part of the day,
Or for many years or stretching eyeles of years.

The early lilacs became part of this child,
And grass and white and red morning-glories, and white and red clover, and the song of the phœbe-bird,
And the Third-month lambs and the sow's pink-faint litter, and the mare's foal and the cow's calf,
And the noisy brood of the barnyard or by the mire of the pondside,
And the fish suspending themselves so curiously below there, and the beautiful curious liquid,
And the water-plants with their graceful flat heads, all became part of him.
His own parents, he that had father'd him and she that had conceiv'd him in her womb and birth'd him,
They gave this child more of themselves than that,
They gave him afterward every day, they became part of him.

Lullaby

Thomas Dekker

Golden slumbers kiss your eyes,
Smiles awake you when you rise.
Sleep, pretty wantons; do not cry,
And I will sing a lullaby:
Rock them, rock them, lullaby.

Care is heavy, therefore sleep you;
You are care, and care must keep you.
Sleep, pretty wantons; do not cry,
And I will sing a lullaby:
Rock them, rock them, lullaby.

Songs of Innocence

William Blake

Introduction

Piping down the valleys wild,
Piping songs of pleasant glee,
On a cloud I saw a child,
And he laughing said to me:

"Pipe a song about a Lamb!"
So I piped with merry chear.
"Piper, pipe that song again"
So I piped, he wept to hear.

"Drop thy pipe, thy happy pipe;
Sing thy songs of happy chear—"
So I sung the same again,
While he wept with joy to hear.

"Piper, sit thee down and write
In a book, that all may read."
So he vanish'd from my sight,
And I pluck'd a hollow reed,

And I made a rural pen,
And I stain'd the water clear,
And I wrote my happy songs
Every child may joy to hear.

The Shepherd

How sweet is the Shepherd's sweet lot!
From the morn to the evening he strays;
He shall follow his sheep all the day,
And his tongue shall be filled with praise.

For he hears the lamb's innocent call,
And he hears the ewe's tender reply;
He is watchful while they are in peace,
For they know when their Shepherd is nigh.

The Ecchoing Green

The Sun does arise,
And make happy the skies;
The merry bells ring
To welcome the Spring;
The sky-lark and thrush,
The birds of the bush,
Sing louder around
To the bells' chearful sound,
While our sports shall be seen
On the Ecchoing Green.

Old John with white hair,
Does laugh away care,
Sitting under the oak,
Among the old folk.
They laugh at our play,
And soon they all say:
"Such, such were the joys
When we all, girls & boys,
In our youth time were seen
On the Ecchoing Green."

Till the little ones, weary,
No more can be merry;
The sun does descend,
And our sports have an end.
Round the laps of their mothers
Many sisters and brothers,
Like birds in their nest,
Are ready for rest,
And sport no more seen,
On the darkening Green.

The Lamb

  Little Lamb, who made thee?
  Dost thou know who made thee?
Gave thee life & bid thee feed,
By the stream & o'er the mead;
Gave thee clothing of delight,
Softest clothing, wooly, bright;
Gave thee such a tender voice,
Making all the vales rejoice?
  Little Lamb, who made thee?
  Dost thou know who made thee?

  Little Lamb, I'll tell thee,
  Little Lamb, I'll tell thee:
He is called by thy name,
For he calls himself a Lamb.
He is meek, & he is mild;
He became a little child.
I a child & thou a lamb,
We are called by his name.
  Little Lamb, God bless thee!
  Little Lamb, God bless thee!

The Little Black Boy

My mother bore me in the southern wild,
And I am black, but O! my soul is white;
White as an angel is the English child,
But I am black as if bereav'd of light.

My mother taught me underneath a tree,
And sitting down before the heat of day,
She took me on her lap and kissed me,
And pointing to the east began to say:

"Look on the rising sun: there God does live,
And gives his light, and gives his heat away;
And flowers and trees and beasts and men recieve
Comfort in morning, joy in the noonday.

"And we are put on earth a little space,
That we may learn to bear the beams of love;
And these black bodies and this sunburnt face
Is but a cloud, and like a shady grove.

"For when our souls have learn'd the heat to bear,
The cloud will vanish: we shall hear his voice,
Saying: 'Come out from the grove, my love & care,
And round my golden tent like lambs rejoice.' "

Thus did my mother say, and kissed me;
And thus I say to little English boy.
When I from black and he from white cloud free,
And round the tent of God like lambs we joy,

I'll shade him from the heat, till he can bear
To lean in joy upon our father's knee;
And then I'll stand and stroke his silver hair,
And be like him, and he will then love me.

The Blossom

Merry Merry Sparrow!
Under leaves so green
A happy Blossom
Sees you swift as arrow
Seek your cradle narrow
Near my Bosom.

Pretty Pretty Robin
Under leaves so green
A happy Blossom
Hears you sobbing, sobbing,
Pretty Pretty Robin,
Near my Bosom.

The Chimney Sweeper

When my mother died I was very young,
And my father sold me while yet my tongue
Could scarcely cry " 'weep! 'weep! 'weep! 'weep!"
So your chimneys I sweep & in soot I sleep.

There's little Tom Dacre, who cried when his head,
That curl'd like a lamb's back, was shav'd: so I said
"Hush, Tom! never mind it, for when your head's bare
You know that the soot cannot spoil your white hair."

And so he was quiet, & that very night,
As Tom was a-sleeping, he had such a sight!
That thousands of sweepers, Dick, Joe, Ned, & Jack,
Were all of them lock'd up in coffins of black.

And by came an Angel who had a bright key,
And he open'd the coffins & set them all free;
Then down a green plain leaping, laughing, they run,
And wash in a river, and shine in the Sun.

Then naked & white, all their bags left behind,
They rise upon clouds and sport in the wind;
And the Angel told Tom, if he'd be a good boy,
He'd have God for his father, & never want joy.

And so Tom awoke; and we rose in the dark,
And got with our bags & our brushes to work.
Tho' the morning was cold, Tom was happy & warm;
So if all do their duty they need not fear harm.

The Little Boy Lost

"Father! father! where are you going?
O do not walk so fast.
Speak, father, speak to your little boy,
Or else I shall be lost."

The night was dark, no father was there;
The child was wet with dew;
The mire was deep, & the child did weep,
And away the vapour flew.

The Little Boy Found

The little boy lost in the lonely fen,
Led by the wand'ring light,
Began to cry; but God ever nigh,
Appear'd like his father in white.

He kissed the child & by the hand led
And to his mother brought,
Who in sorrow pale, thro' the lonely dale,
Her little boy weeping sought.

Laughing Song

When the green woods laugh, with the voice of joy,
And the dimpling stream runs laughing by;
When the air does laugh with our merry wit,
And the green hill laughs with the noise of it;

When the meadows laugh with lively green,
And the grasshopper laughs in the merry scene,
When Mary and Susan and Emily
With their sweet round mouths sing "Ha, Ha, He!"

When the painted birds laugh in the shade,
Where our table with cherries and nuts is spread,
Come live & be merry and join with me,
To sing the sweet chorus of "Ha, Ha, He!"

A Cradle Song

Sweet dreams form a shade
O'er my lovely infant's head;
Sweet dreams of pleasant streams
By happy, silent, moony beams.

Sweet sleep with soft down
Weave thy brows an infant crown.
Sweet sleep, Angel mild,
Hover o'er my happy child.

Sweet smiles in the night
Hover over my delight;
Sweet smiles, Mother's smiles,
All the livelong night beguiles.

Sweet moans, dovelike sighs,
Chase not slumber from thy eyes.
Sweet moans, sweeter smiles,
All the dovelike moans beguiles.

Sleep sleep, happy child,
All creation slept and smil'd;
Sleep sleep, happy sleep,
While o'er thee thy mother weep.

Sweet babe, in thy face
Holy image I can trace.
Sweet babe, once like thee,
Thy maker lay and wept for me,

Wept for me, for thee, for all,
When he was an infant small.
Thou his image ever see,
Heavenly face that smiles on thee,

Smiles on thee, on me, on all;
Who became an infant small.
Infant smiles are his own smiles;
Heaven & earth to peace beguiles.

The Divine Image

To Mercy, Pity, Peace, and Love,
All pray in their distress;
And to these virtues of delight
Return their thankfulness.

For Mercy, Pity, Peace, and Love
Is God, our father dear,
And Mercy, Pity, Peace, and Love
Is Man, his child and care.

For Mercy has a human heart,
Pity, a human face,
And Love, the human form divine,
And Peace, the human dress.

Then every man, of every clime,
That prays in his distress,
Prays to the human form divine
Love, Mercy, Pity, Peace.

And all must love the human form,
In heathen, turk, or jew;
Where Mercy, Love & Pity dwell
There God is dwelling too.

Holy Thursday

'Twas on a Holy Thursday, their innocent faces clean,
The children walking two & two, in red & blue & green,
Grey-headed beadles walk'd before, with wands as white as snow,
Till into the high dome of Paul's they like Thames' waters flow.

O what a multitude they seem'd, these flowers of London town!
Seated in companies they sit with radiance all their own.
The hum of multitudes was there, but multitudes of lambs,
Thousands of little boys & girls raising their innocent hands.

Now like a mighty wind they raise to heaven the voice of song,
Or like harmonious thunderings the seats of heaven among.
Beneath them sit the aged men, wise guardians of the poor;
Then cherish pity, lest you drive an angel from your door.

Night

The sun descending in the west,
The evening star does shine;
The birds are silent in their nest,
And I must seek for mine.
The moon like a flower,
In heavens high bower,
With silent delight
Sits and smiles on the night.

Farewell, green fields and happy groves,
Where flocks have took delight;
Where lambs have nibbled, silent moves
The feet of angels bright;
Unseen they pour blessing,
And joy without ceasing,
On each bud and blossom,
And each sleeping bosom.

They look in every thoughtless nest,
Where birds are cover'd warm;
They visit caves of every beast,
To keep them all from harm;
If they see any weeping
That should have been sleeping
They pour sleep on their head
And sit down by their bed.

When wolves and tygers howl for prey,
They pitying stand and weep;
Seeking to drive their thirst away,
And keep them from the sheep.
But if they rush dreadful,
The angels, most heedful,
Recieve each mild spirit,
New worlds to inherit.

And there the lion's ruddy eyes
Shall flow with tears of gold,
And pitying the tender cries,
And walking round the fold,
Saying "Wrath, by his meekness,
And by his health, sickness
Is driven away
From our immortal day.

"And now beside thee, bleating lamb,
I can lie down and sleep;
Or think on him who bore thy name,
Graze after thee and weep.
For, wash'd in life's river,
My bright mane for ever
Shall shine like the gold
As I guard o'er the fold."

Spring

Sound the Flute!
Now it's mute.
Birds delight
Day and Night;
Nightingale
In the dale,
Lark in Sky
Merrily,
Merrily, Merrily, to welcome in the Year.

Little Boy,
Full of joy;
Little Girl,
Sweet and small;
Cock does crow,
So do you;
Merry voice,
Infant noise,
Merrily, Merrily, to welcome in the Year.

Little Lamb,
Here I am;
Come and lick
My white neck;
Let me pull
Your soft Wool;
Let me kiss
Your soft face:
Merrily, Merrily, we welcome in the Year.

Nurse's Song

When the voices of children are heard on the green
And laughing is heard on the hill,
My heart is at rest within my breast,
And every thing else is still.

"Then come home, my children, the sun is gone down
And the dews of night arise;
Come, come, leave off play, and let us away
Till the morning appears in the skies."

"No, no, let us play, for it is yet day
And we cannot go to sleep;
Besides, in the sky, the little birds fly
And the hills are all covered with sheep."

"Well, well, go & play till the light fades away
And then go home to bed."
The little ones leaped & shouted & laugh'd
And all the hills ecchoed.

Infant Joy

"I have no name:
I am but two days old."
What shall I call thee?
"I happy am,
Joy is my name."
Sweet joy befall thee!

Pretty joy!
Sweet joy but two days old,
Sweet joy I call thee:
Thou dost smile,
I sing the while,
Sweet joy befall thee!

A Dream

Once a dream did weave a shade
O'er my Angel-guarded bed,
That an Emmet lost its way
Where on grass methought I lay.

Troubled, 'wilder'd and folorn,
Dark, benighted, travel-worn,
Over many a tangled spray,
All heart-broke I heard her say:

"O my children! do they cry?
Do they hear their father sigh?
Now they look abroad to see:
Now return and weep for me."

Pitying, I drop'd a tear;
But I saw a glow-worm near,
Who replied: "What wailing wight
Calls the watchman of the night?

"I am set to light the ground,
While the beetle goes his round:
Follow now the beetle's hum;
Little wanderer, hie thee home."

On Another's Sorrow

Can I see another's woe,
And not be in sorrow too?
Can I see another's grief,
And not seek for kind relief?

Can I see a falling tear,
And not feel my sorrow's share?
Can a father see his child
Weep, nor be with sorrow fill'd?

Can a mother sit and hear
An infant groan an infant fear?
No, no! never can it be!
Never, never can it be!

And can he who smiles on all
Hear the wren with sorrows small,
Hear the small bird's grief & care,
Hear the woes that infants bear,

And not sit beside the nest,
Pouring pity in their breast;
And not sit the cradle near,
Weeping tear on infant's tear;

And not sit both night & day,
Wiping all our tears away?
O! no! never can it be!
Never, never can it be!

He doth give his joy to all;
He becomes an infant small;
He becomes a man of woe;
He doth feel the sorrow too.

Think not thou canst sigh a sigh
And thy maker is not by;
Think not thou canst weep a tear
And thy maker is not near.

O! he gives to us his joy
That our grief he may destroy;
Till our grief is fled & gone
He doth sit by us and moan.

Songs of Experience

William Blake

Introduction

Hear the voice of the Bard!
Who Present, Past, & Future sees
Whose ears have heard,
The Holy Word,
That walk'd among the ancient trees.

Calling the lapsed Soul
And weeping in the evening dew:
That might controll,
The starry pole;
And fallen fallen light renew!

O Earth O Earth return!
Arise from out the dewy grass;
Night is worn,
And the morn
Rises from the slumberous mass.

Turn away no more:
Why wilt thou turn away
The starry floor
The watry shore
Is giv'n thee till the break of day

Earth's Answer

Earth rais'd up her head,
From the darkness dread & drear.
Her light fled:
Stony dread!
And her locks cover'd with grey despair.

Prison'd on watry shore
Starry Jealousy does keep my den
Cold and hoar
Weeping o'er
I hear the Father of the ancient men

Selfish father of men
Cruel jealous selfish fear
Can delight
Chain'd in night
The virgins of youth and morning bear.

Does spring hide its joy
When buds and blossoms grow?
Does the sower!
Sow by night?
Or the plowman in darkness plow!

Break this heavy chain,
That does freeze my bones around
Selfish! vain!

Eternal bane!
That free Love with bondage bound.

The Clod & the Pebble

Love seeketh not Itself to please,
Nor for itself hath any care;
But for another gives its ease,
And builds a Heaven in Hells despair.

So sang a little Clod of Clay,
Trodden with the cattles feet:
But a Pebble of the brook,
Warbled out these metres meet.

Love seeketh only Self to please,
To bind another to Its delight:
Joys in anothers loss of ease,
And builds a Hell in Heavens despite.

Holy Thursday

Is this a holy thing to see,
In a rich and fruitful land,
Babes reduced to misery,
Fed with cold and usurous hand?

Is that trembling cry a song!
Can it be a song of joy?

And so many children poor,
It is a land of poverty!

And their sun does never shine.
And their fields are bleak & bare.
And their ways are fill'd with thorns
It is eternal winter there.

For where-e'er the sun does shine,
And where-e'er the rain does fall:
Babe can never hunger there,
Nor poverty the mind appall.

The Little Girl Lost

In futurity
I prophetic see,
That the earth from sleep,
(Grave the sentence deep)

Shall arise and seek
For her maker meek:
And the desart wild
Become a garden mild.

In the southern clime,
Where the summers prime,
Never fades away;
Lovely Lyca lay.

Seven summers old
Lovely Lyca told.
She had wanderd long,
Hearing wild birds song.

Sweet sleep come to me
Underneath this tree;
Do father, mother weep.
Where can Lyca sleep.

Lost in desart wild
Is your little child.
How can Lyca sleep,
If her mother weep.

If her heart does ake,
Then let Lyca wake;
If my mother sleep,
Lyca shall not weep.

Frowning frowning night,
O'er this desart bright,
Let thy moon arise,
While I close my eyes.

Sleeping Lyca lay;
While the beasts of prey,
Come from caverns deep,
View'd the maid asleep.

The kingly lion stood
And the virgin view'd,

Then he gambold round
O'er the hallowd ground;

Leopards, tygers play,
Round her as she lay;
While the lion old,
Bow'd his mane of gold.

And her bosom lick,
And upon her neck,
From his eyes of flame,
Ruby tears there came;

While the lioness,
Loos'd her slender dress,
And naked they convey'd
To caves the sleeping maid.

The Little Girl Found

All the night in woe,
Lyca's parents go:
Over vallies deep,
While the desarts weep.

Tired and woe-begone,
Hoarse with making moan:
Arm in arm seven days,
They trac'd the desart ways.

Seven nights they sleep,
Among shadows deep:
And dream they see their child
Starv'd in desart wild.

Pale thro' pathless ways
The fancied image strays,
Famish'd, weeping, weak
With hollow piteous shriek

Rising from unrest,
The trembling woman prest,
With feet of weary woe;
She could no further go.

In his arms he bore,
Her arm'd with sorrow sore;
Till before their way,
A couching lion lay.

Turning back was vain,
Soon his heavy mane,
Bore them to the ground;
Then he stalk'd around,

Smelling to his prey.
But their fears allay,
When he licks their hands;
And silent by them stands.

They look upon his eyes.
Fill'd with deep surprise

And wondering behold,
A spirit arm'd in gold.

On his head a crown
On his shoulders down,
Flow'd his golden hair.
Gone was all their care.

Follow me he said,
Weep not for the maid;
In my palace deep,
Lyca lies asleep.

Then they followed,
Where the vision led:
And saw their sleeping child
Among tygers wild.

To this day they dwell
In a lonely dell
Nor fear the wolvish howl,
Nor the lions growl.

The Chimney Sweeper

A little black thing among the snow:
Crying weep, weep, in notes of woe!
Where are thy father & mother? say?
They are both gone up to the church to pray.

Because I was happy upon the heath,
And smil'd among the winters snow:
They clothed me in the clothes of death,
And taught me to sing the notes of woe.

And because I am happy, & dance & sing,
They think they have done me no injury:
And are gone to praise God & his Priest & King
Who make up a heaven of our misery.

Nurses Song

When the voices of children, are heard on the green
And whisprings are in the dale:
The days of my youth rise fresh in my mind,
My face turns green and pale.

Then come home my children, the sun is gone down
And the dews of night arise

Your spring & your day, are wasted in play
And your winter and night in disguise.

The Sick Rose

O Rose thou art sick.
The invisible worm,
That flies in the night
In the howling storm:

Has found out thy bed
Of crimson joy:
And his dark secret love
Does thy life destroy.

The Fly

Little Fly
Thy summers play,
My thoughtless hand
Has brush'd away.

Am not I
A fly like thee?
Or art not thou
A man like me?

For I dance
And drink & sing:

Till some blind hand
Shall brush my wing.

If thought is life
And strength & breath
And the want
Of thought is death;

Then am I
A happy fly,
If I live,
Or if I die.

The Angel

I Dreamt a Dream! what can it mean?
And that I was a maiden Queen:
Guarded by an Angel mild:
Witless woe, was ne'er beguil'd!

And I wept both night and day
And he wip'd my tears away
And I wept both day and night
And hid from him my hearts delight

So he took his wings and fled:
Then the morn blush'd rosy red:
I dried my tears & armed my fears,
With ten thousand shields and spears.

Soon my Angel came again;
I was arm'd, he came in vain:
For the time of youth was fled
And grey hairs were on my head.

The Tyger

Tyger Tyger, burning bright,
In the forests of the night;
What immortal hand or eye,
Could frame thy fearful symmetry?

In what distant deeps or skies.
Burnt the fire of thine eyes?
On what wings dare he aspire?
What the hand, dare sieze the fire?

And what shoulder, & what art,
Could twist the sinews of thy heart?
And when thy heart began to beat,
What dread hand? & what dread feet?

What the hammer? what the chain,
In what furnace was thy brain?
What the anvil? what dread grasp,
Dare its deadly terrors clasp!

When the stars threw down their spears
And water'd heaven with their tears:

Did he smile his work to see?
Did he who made the Lamb make thee?

Tyger Tyger burning bright,
In the forests of the night:
What immortal hand or eye,
Dare frame thy fearful symmetry?

My Pretty Rose Tree

A flower was offerd to me;
Such a flower as May never bore.
But I said I've a Pretty Rose-tree:
And I passed the sweet flower o'er.

Then I went to my Pretty Rose-tree;
To tend her by day and by night.
But my Rose turnd away with jealousy:
And her thorns were my only delight.

Ah! Sun-flower

Ah Sun-flower! weary of time,
Who countest the steps of the Sun:
Seeking after that sweet golden clime
Where the travellers journey is done.

Where the Youth pined away with desire,
And the pale Virgin shrouded in snow:

Arise from their graves and aspire,
Where my Sun-flower wishes to go.

The Lilly

The modest Rose puts forth a thorn:
The humble Sheep, a threatning horn:
While the Lilly white, shall in Love delight,
Nor a thorn nor a threat stain her beauty bright.

The Garden of Love

I went to the Garden of Love,
And saw what I never had seen:
A Chapel was built in the midst,
Where I used to play on the green.

And the gates of this Chapel were shut,
And Thou shalt not, writ over the door;
So I turn'd to the Garden of Love,
That so many sweet flowers bore.

And I saw it was filled with graves,
And tomb-stones where flowers should be:
And Priests in black gowns, were walking their rounds,
And binding with briars, my joys & desires.

The Little Vagabond

Dear Mother, dear Mother, the Church is cold,
But the Ale-house is healthy & pleasant & warm;
Besides I can tell where I am use'd well,
Such usage in heaven will never do well.

But if at the Church they would give us some Ale,
And a pleasant fire, our souls to regale;
We'd sing and we'd pray, all the live-long day;
Nor ever once wish from the Church to stray,

Then the Parson might preach & drink & sing.
And we'd be as happy as birds in the spring:
And modest dame Lurch, who is always at Church,
Would not have bandy children nor fasting nor birch.

And God like a father rejoicing to see,
His children as pleasant and happy as he:
Would have no more quarrel with the Devil or the Barrel
But kiss him & give him both drink and apparel.

London

I wander thro' each charter'd street,
Near where the charter'd Thames does flow
And mark in every face I meet
Marks of weakness, marks of woe.

In every cry of every Man,
In every Infants cry of fear,
In every voice: in every ban,
The mind-forg'd manacles I hear

How the Chimney-sweepers cry
Every blackning Church appalls,
And the hapless Soldiers sigh
Runs in blood down Palace walls

But most thro' midnight streets I hear
How the youthful Harlots curse
Blasts the new-born Infants tear
And blights with plagues the Marriage hearse

The Human Abstract

Pity would be no more,
If we did not make somebody Poor:
And Mercy no more could be,
If all were as happy as we;

And mutual fear brings peace;
Till the selfish loves increase.
Then Cruelty knits a snare,
And spreads his baits with care.

He sits down with holy fears,
And waters the ground with tears:
Then Humility takes its root
Underneath his foot.

Soon spreads the dismal shade
Of Mystery over his head;
And the Catterpiller and Fly,
Feed on the Mystery.

And it bears the fruit of Deceit,
Ruddy and sweet to eat;
And the Raven his nest has made
In its thickest shade.

The Gods of the earth and sea,
Sought thro' Nature to find this Tree

But their search was all in vain:
There grows one in the Human Brain

Infant Sorrow

My mother groand! my father wept.
Into the dangerous world I leapt:
Helpless, naked, piping loud;
Like a fiend hid in a cloud.

Struggling in my fathers hands:
Striving against my swadling bands:
Bound and weary I thought best
To sulk upon my mothers breast.

A Poison Tree

I was angry with my friend;
I told my wrath, my wrath did end.
I was angry with my foe:
I told it not, my wrath did grow.

And I waterd it in fears,
Night & morning with my tears:
And I sunned it with smiles,
And with soft deceitful wiles.

And it grew both day and night.
Till it bore an apple bright.

And my foe beheld it shine,
And he knew that it was mine.

And into my garden stole,
When the night had veild the pole;
In the morning glad I see;
My foe outstretchd beneath the tree.

A Little Boy Lost

Nought loves another as itself
Nor venerates another so.
Nor is it possible to Thought
A greater than itself to know:

And Father, how can I love you,
Or any of my brothers more?
I love you like the little bird
That picks up crumbs around the door.

The Priest sat by and heard the child.
In trembling zeal he siez'd his hair:
He led him by his little coat:
And all admir'd the Priestly care.

And standing on the altar high,
Lo what a fiend is here! said he:
One who sets reasons up for judge
Of our most holy Mystery.

The weeping child could not be heard.
The weeping parents wept in vain:
They strip'd him to his little shirt.
And bound him in an iron chain.

And burn'd him in a holy place,
Where many had been burn'd before:
The weeping parents wept in vain.
Are such things done on Albions shore.

A Little Girl Lost

Children of the future Age,
Reading this indignant page:
Know that in a former time,
Love! sweet Love! was thought a crime.

In the Age of Gold,
Free from winters cold:
Youth and maiden bright,
To the holy light,
Naked in the sunny beams delight.

Once a youthful pair
Fill'd with softest care:
Met in garden bright,
Where the holy light,
Had just removd the curtains of the night.

There in rising day,
On the grass they play:

Parents were afar:
Strangers came not near:
And the maiden soon forgot her fear.

Tired with kisses sweet
They agree to meet,
When the silent sleep
Waves o'er heavens deep;
And the weary tired wanderers weep.

To her father white
Came the maiden bright:
But his loving look,
Like the holy book,
All her tender limbs with terror shook.

Ona! pale and weak!
To thy father speak:
O the trembling fear!
O the dismal care!
That shakes the blossoms of my hoary hair

To Tirzah

Whate'er is Born of Mortal Birth,
Must be consumed with the Earth
To rise from Generation free;
Then what have I to do with thee?

The Sexes sprung from Shame & Pride
Blow'd in the morn: in evening died
But Mercy changd Death into Sleep;
The Sexes rose to work & weep.

Thou Mother of my Mortal part.
With cruelty didst mould my Heart.
And with false self-decieving tears,
Didst bind my Nostrils Eyes & Ears.

Didst close my tongue in senseless clay
And me to Mortal Life betray:
The Death of Jesus set me free,
Then what have I to do with thee?

The School Boy

I love to rise in a summer morn,
When the birds sing on every tree;
The distant huntsman winds his horn,
And the sky-lark sings with me.
O! what sweet company.

But to go to school in a summer morn,
O! it drives all joy away;
Under a cruel eye outworn,
The little ones spend the day,
In sighing and dismay.

Ah! then at times I drooping sit,
And spend many an anxious hour.
Nor in my book can I take delight,
Nor sit in learnings bower,
Worn thro' with the dreary shower.

How can the bird that is born for joy,
Sit in a cage and sing.
How can a child when fears annoy,
But droop his tender wing,
And forget his youthful spring?

O! father & mother, if buds are nip'd,
And blossoms blown away,

And if the tender plants are strip'd
Of their joy in the springing day,
By sorrow and cares dismay,

How shall the summer arise in joy.
Or the summer fruits appear,
Or how shall we gather what griefs destroy
Or bless the mellowing year,
When the blasts of winter appear.

The Voice of the Ancient Bard

Youth of delight come hither:
And see the opening morn,
Image of truth new born.
Doubt is fled & clouds of reason
Dark disputes & artful teazing.
Folly is an endless maze,
Tangled roots perplex her ways,
How many have fallen there!
They stumble all night over bones of the dead;
And feel they know not what but care;
And wish to lead others when they should be led.

A Divine Image

Cruelty has a Human Heart,
And Jealousy a Human Face;
Terror, the Human Form Divine,
And Secrecy, the Human Dress.

The Human Dress is forged Iron,
The Human Form a fiery Forge,
The Human Face, a Furnace seal'd,
The Human Heart its hungry Gorge.

STORIES AND EXCERPTS

"The Bohemian Girl," one of the many great short works by the American writer Willa Cather (1873–1947), addresses the value of a mother to her two sons. The Tenant of Wildfell Hall, *one of the two novels by Anne Brontë (1820–1849), the lesser-known but equally talented sister of Charlotte and Emily, tells the story of a most memorable mother, Helen Graham; presented here is a chapter that captures a conversation on the dilemmas of child rearing. From* Little Women, *by Louisa May Alcott (1832–1888), we have Marmee, one of fiction's most adored mothers, and a few of her unforgettable lessons for Meg, Jo, Beth, and Amy. Also from Louisa May Alcott is "Huckleberries," a chapter from* Little Men—*Alcott's companion volume to* Little Women—*which focuses on Jo and her boys.*

The Bohemian Girl

Willa Cather

The transcontinental express swung along the windings of the Sand River Valley, and in the rear seat of the observation car a young man sat greatly at his ease, not in the least discomfited by the fierce sunlight which beat in upon his brown face and neck and strong back. There was a look of relaxation and of great passivity about his broad shoulders, which seemed almost too heavy until he stood up and squared them. He wore a pale flannel shirt and a blue silk necktie with loose ends. His trousers were wide and belted at the waist, and his short sack coat hung open. His heavy shoes had seen good service. His reddish-brown hair, like his clothes, had a foreign cut. He had deep-set, dark blue eyes under heavy reddish eyebrows. His face was kept clean only by close shaving, and even the sharpest razor left a glint of yellow in the smooth brown of his skin. His teeth and the palms of his hands were very white. His head, which looked hard and stubborn, lay indolently in the green cushion of the wicker chair, and as he looked out at the ripe summer country a teasing, not unkindly smile played over his lips. Once, as he basked thus comfortably, a quick light flashed in his eyes, curiously dilating the pupils, and his mouth became a hard, straight line, gradually relaxing into its former smile of rather kindly mockery. He told himself, apparently, that there was no point in getting excited; and he seemed a master hand at taking his ease when he could. Neither the sharp whistle of the locomotive nor the brakeman's call disturbed him. It was not until after the train had stopped that he rose, put on a Panama hat, took from the rack a small valise and a flute case, and stepped deliberately to the station platform. The baggage was already unloaded, and the stranger presented a check for a battered sole-leather steamer trunk.

"Can you keep it here for a day or two?" he asked the agent. "I may send for it, and I may not."

"Depends on whether you like the country, I suppose?" demanded the agent in a challenging tone.

"Just so."

The agent shrugged his shoulders, looked scornfully at the small trunk, which was marked. "N.E.," and handed out a claim check without further comment. The stranger watched him as he caught one end of the trunk and dragged it into the express room. The agent's manner seemed to remind him of something amusing. "Doesn't seem to be a very big place," he remarked, looking about.

"It's big enough for us," snapped the agent, as he banged the trunk into a corner.

That remark, apparently, was what Nils Ericson had wanted. He chuckled quietly as he took a leather strap from his pocket and swung his valise around his shoulder. Then he settled his Panama securely on his head, turned up his trousers, tucked the flute case under his arm, and started off across the fields. He gave the town, as he would have said, a wide berth, and cut through a great fenced pasture, emerging, when he rolled under the barbed wire at the farther corner, upon a white dusty road which ran straight up from the river valley to the high prairies, where the ripe wheat stood yellow and the tin roofs and weathercocks were twinkling in the fierce sunlight. By the time Nils had done three miles, the sun was sinking and the farm wagons on their way home from town came rattling by, covering him with dust and making him sneeze. When one of the farmers pulled up and offered to give him a lift, he clambered in willingly. The driver was a thin, grizzled old man with a long lean neck and a foolish sort of beard, like a goat's. "How fur ye goin'?" he asked, as he clucked to his horses and started off.

"Do you go by the Ericson place?"

"Which Ericson?" The old man drew in his reins as if he expected to stop again.

"Preacher Ericson's."

"Oh, the Old Lady Ericson's!" He turned and looked at Nils. "La, me! If you're goin' out there you might 'a' rid out in the automobile. That's a pity, now. The Old Lady Ericson was in town with her auto. You might 'a' heard it snortin' anywhere about the post-office er the butcher shop."

"Has she a motor?" asked the stranger absently.

" 'Deed an' she has! She runs into town every night about this time for her mail and meat for supper. Some folks say she's afraid her auto won't get exercise enough, but I say that's jealousy."

"Aren't there any other motors about here?"

"Oh, yes! we have fourteen in all. But nobody else gets around like the Old Lady Ericson. She's out, rain er shine, over the whole county, chargin' into town and out amongst her farms, an' up to her sons' places. Sure you ain't goin' to the wrong place?" He craned his neck and looked at Nils' flute case with eager curiosity. "The old woman ain't got any piany that I knows on. Olaf, he has a grand. His wife's musical; took lessons in Chicago."

"I'm going up there tomorrow," said Nils imperturbably. He saw that the driver took him for a piano tuner.

"Oh, I see!" The old man screwed up his eyes mysteriously. He was a little dashed by the stranger's noncommunicativeness, but he soon broke out again.

"I'm one o' Miss Ericson's tenants. Look after one of her places. I did own the place myself oncet, but I lost it a while back, in the bad years just after the World's Fair. Just as well, too, I say. Lets you out o' payin' taxes. The Ericsons do own most of the county now. I remember the old preacher's fav'rite text used to be, 'To them that hath shall be given.' They've spread something wonderful—run over this here country like bindweed. But I ain't one that begretches it to 'em. Folks is entitled to what they kin git; and they're hustlers. Olaf, he's in the Legislature now, and a likely man fur Congress. Listen, if that ain't the old woman comin' now. Want I should stop her?"

Nils shook his head. He heard the deep chug-chug of a motor vibrating steadily in the clear twilight behind them. The pale lights of the car swam over the hill, and the old man slapped his reins and turned clear out of the road, ducking his head at the first of three angry snorts from behind. The motor was running at a hot, even speed, and passed without turning an inch from its course. The driver was a stalwart woman who sat at ease in the front seat and drove her car bareheaded. She left a cloud of dust and a trail of gasoline behind her. Her tenant threw back his head and sneezed.

"Whew! I sometimes say I'd as lief be *before* Mrs. Ericson as behind her. She does beat all! Nearly seventy, and never lets another soul touch that car. Puts it into commission herself every morning, and keeps it tuned up by the hitch-bar all day. I never stop work for a drink o' water that I don't hear her a-churnin' up the road. I reckon her darter-in-laws never sets down easy nowadays. Never know when she'll pop in. Mis' Otto, she says to me: 'We're so afraid that thing'll blow up and do Ma some injury yet, she's so turrible venturesome.' Says I: 'I wouldn't stew, Mis' Otto; the old lady'll drive that car to the funeral of every darter-in-law she's got.' That was after the old woman had jumped a turrible bad culvert."

The stranger heard vaguely what the old man was saying. Just now he was experiencing something very much like homesickness, and he was wondering what had brought it about. The mention of a name or two, perhaps; the rattle of a wagon along a dusty road; the rank, resinous smell of sunflowers and ironweed, which the night damp brought up from the draws and low places; perhaps, more than all, the dancing lights of the motor that had plunged by. He squared his shoulders with a comfortable sense of strength.

The wagon, as it jolted westward, climbed a pretty steady up-grade. The country, receding from the rough river valley, swelled more and more gently, as if it had been smoothed out by the wind. On one of the last of the rugged ridges, at the end of a branch road, stood a grim square house with a tin roof and double porches. Behind the house stretched a row of broken, wind-racked poplars, and down the hill slope to the left straggled the sheds and stables. The old man stopped his horses where the Ericsons' road branched across a dry sand creek that wound about the foot of the hill.

"That's the old lady's place. Want I should drive in?" "No, thank you. I'll roll out here. Much obliged to you. Good night."

His passenger stepped down over the front wheel, and the old man drove on reluctantly, looking back as if he would like to see how the stranger would be received.

As Nils was crossing the dry creek he heard the restive tramp of a horse coming toward him down the hill. Instantly he flashed out of the road and stood behind a thicket of wild plum bushes that grew in the sandy bed. Peering through the dusk, he saw a light horse, under tight rein, descending the hill at a sharp walk. The rider was a slender woman—barely visible against the dark hillside—wearing an old-fashioned derby hat and a long riding skirt. She sat lightly in the saddle, with her chin high, and seemed to be looking into the distance. As she passed the plum thicket her horse snuffed the air and shied. She struck him, pulling him in sharply, with an angry exclamation, *"Blázne!"* in Bohemian. Once in the main road, she let him out into a lope, and they soon emerged upon the crest of high land, where they moved along the skyline, silhouetted against the band of faint colour that lingered in the west. This horse and rider, with their free, rhythmical gallop, were the only moving things to be seen on the face of the flat country. They seemed, in the last sad light of evening, not to be there accidentally, but as an inevitable detail of the landscape.

Nils watched them until they had shrunk to a mere moving speck against the sky, then he crossed the sand creek and climbed the hill. When he reached the gate the front of the house was dark, but a light was shining from the side windows. The pigs were squealing in the hog corral, and Nils could see a tall boy, who carried two big wooden buckets, moving about among them. Halfway between the barn and the house, the windmill wheezed lazily. Following the path that ran around to the back porch, Nils stopped to look through the screen door into the lamplit kitchen. The kitchen was the largest room in the house; Nils remembered that his older brothers used to give dances there when he was a boy. Beside the stove stood a little girl with two light yellow braids and a broad, flushed face, peering anxiously into a frying pan. In the dining-room beyond, a large, broad-shouldered woman was moving about the table. She walked with an active, springy step. Her face was heavy and florid, almost without wrinkles, and her hair was black at seventy. Nils felt proud of her as he watched her deliberate activity; never a momentary hesitation, or a movement that did not tell. He waited until she came out into the kitchen and, brushing the child aside, took her place at the stove. Then he tapped on the screen door and entered.

"It's nobody but Nils, Mother. I expect you weren't looking for me."

Mrs. Ericson turned away from the stove and stood staring at him. "Bring the lamp, Hilda, and let me look."

Nils laughed and unslung his valise. "What's the matter, Mother? Don't you know me?"

Mrs. Ericson put down the lamp. "You must be Nils. You don't look very different, anyway."

"Nor you, Mother. You hold your own. Don't you wear glasses yet?"

"Only to read by. Where's your trunk, Nils?"

"Oh, I left that in town. I thought it might not be convenient for you to have company so near threshing-time."

"Don't be foolish, Nils." Mrs. Ericson turned back to the stove. "I don't thresh now. I hitched the wheat land onto the next farm and have a tenant. Hilda, take some hot water up to the company room, and go call little Eric."

The two-haired child, who had been standing in mute amazement, took up the tea-kettle and withdrew, giving Nils a long, admiring look from the door of the kitchen stairs.

"Who's the youngster?" Nils asked, dropping down on the bench behind the kitchen stove.

"One of your Cousin Henrik's."

"How long has Cousin Henrik been dead?"

"Six years. There are two boys. One stays with Peter and one with Anders. Olaf is their guardeen."

There was a clatter of pails on the porch, and a tall, lanky boy peered wonderingly in through the screen door. He had a fair, gentle face and big grey eyes, and wisps of soft yellow hair hung down under his cap. Nils sprang up and pulled him into the kitchen, hugging him and slapping him on the shoulders. "Well, if it isn't my kid! Look at the size of him! Don't you know me, Eric?"

The boy reddened under his sunburn and freckles, and hung his head. "I guess it's Nils," he said shyly.

"You're a good guesser," laughed Nils giving the lad's hand a swing. To himself he was thinking: "That's why the little girl looked so friendly. He's taught her to like me. He was only six when I went away, and he's remembered for twelve years."

Eric stood fumbling with his cap and smiling. "You look just like I thought you would," he ventured.

"Go wash your hands, Eric," called Mrs. Ericson. "I've got cob corn for supper, Nils. You used to like it. I guess you don't get much of that in the old country. Here's Hilda; she'll take you up to your room. You'll want to get the dust off you before you eat."

Mrs. Ericson went into the dining-room to lay another plate, and the little girl came up and nodded to Nils as if to let him know that his room was ready. He put out his hand and she took it, with a startled glance up at his face. Little Eric dropped his towel, threw an arm about Nils and one about Hilda, gave them a clumsy squeeze, and then stumbled out to the porch.

During supper Nils heard exactly how much land each of his eight grown brothers farmed, how their crops were coming on, and how much livestock they were feeding. His mother watched him narrowly as she talked. "You've got better looking, Nils," she remarked abruptly, whereupon he grinned and the children giggled. Eric, although he was eighteen and as tall as Nils, was always accounted a child, being the last of so many sons. His face seemed childlike, too, Nils thought, and he had the open, wandering eyes of a little boy. All the others had been men at his age.

After supper Nils went out to the front porch and sat down on the step to smoke a pipe. Mrs. Ericson drew a rocking-chair up near him and began to knit busily. It was one of the few Old World customs she had kept up, for she could not bear to sit with idle hands.

"Where's little Eric, Mother?"

"He's helping Hilda with the dishes. He does it of his own will; I don't like a boy to be too handy about the house."

"He seems like a nice kid."

"He's very obedient."

Nils smiled a little in the dark. It was just as well to shift the line of conversation. "What are you knitting there, Mother?"

"Baby stockings. The boys keep me busy." Mrs. Ericson chuckled and clicked her needles.

"How many grandchildren have you?"

"Only thirty-one now. Olaf lost his three. They were sickly, like their mother."

"I supposed he had a second crop by this time!"

"His second wife has no children. She's too proud. She tears about on horseback all the time. But she'll get caught up with, yet. She sets herself very high, though nobody knows what for. They were low enough Bohemians she came of. I never thought much of Bohemians; always drinking."

Nils puffed away at his pipe in silence, and Mrs. Ericson knitted on. In a few moments she added grimly: "She was down here tonight, just before you came. She'd like to quarrel with me and come between me and Olaf, but I don't give her the chance. I suppose you'll be bringing a wife home some day."

"I don't know. I've never thought much about it."

"Well, perhaps it's best as it is," suggested Mrs. Ericson hopefully. "You'd never be contented tied down to the land. There was roving blood in your father's family, and it's come out in you. I expect your own way of life suits you best." Mrs. Ericson had dropped into a blandly agreeable tone which Nils well remembered. It seemed to amuse him a good deal and his white teeth flashed behind his pipe. His mother's strategies had always diverted him, even when he was a boy—they were so flimsy and patent, so illy proportioned to her vigor and force. "They've been waiting to see which way I'd jump," he reflected. He felt that Mrs. Ericson was pondering his case deeply as she sat clicking her needles.

"I don't suppose you've ever got used to steady work," she went on presently. "Men ain't apt to if they roam around too long. It's a pity you didn't come back the year after the World's Fair. Your father picked up a good bit of land cheap then, in the hard times, and I expect maybe he'd have give you a farm. It's too bad you put off comin' back so long, for I always thought he meant to do something by you."

Nils laughed and shook the ashes out of his pipe. "I'd have missed a lot if I had come back then. But I'm sorry I didn't get back to see father."

"Well, I suppose we have to miss things at one end or the other. Perhaps you are as well satisfied with your own doings, now, as you'd have been with a farm," said Mrs. Ericson reassuringly.

"Land's a good thing to have," Nils commented, as he lit another match and sheltered it with his hand.

His mother looked sharply at his face until the match burned out. "Only when you stay on it!" she hastened to say.

Eric came round the house by the path just then, and Nils rose, with a yawn. "Mother, if you don't mind, Eric and I will take a little tramp before bedtime. It will make me sleep."

"Very well; only don't stay long. I'll sit up and wait for you. I like to lock up myself."

Nils put his hand on Eric's shoulder, and the two tramped down the hill and across the sand creek into the dusty highroad beyond. Neither spoke. They swung along at an even gait, Nils puffing at his pipe.

There was no moon, and the white road and the wide fields lay faint in the starlight. Over everything was darkness and thick silence, and the smell of dust and sunflowers. The brothers followed the road for a mile or more without finding a place to sit down. Finally, Nils perched on a stile over the wire fence, and Eric sat on the lower step.

"I began to think you never would come back, Nils," said the boy softly.

"Didn't I promise you I would?"

"Yes; but people don't bother about promises they make to babies. Did you really know you were going away for good when you went to Chicago with the cattle that time?"

"I thought it very likely, if I could make my way."

"I don't see how you did it, Nils. Not many fellows could." Eric rubbed his shoulder against his brother's knee.

"The hard thing was leaving home—you and father. It was easy enough, once I got beyond Chicago. Of course I got awful homesick; used to cry myself to sleep. But I'd burned my bridges."

"You had always wanted to go, hadn't you?"

"Always. Do you still sleep in our little room? Is that cottonwood still by the window?"

Eric nodded eagerly and smiled up at his brother in the grey darkness.

"You remember how we always said the leaves were whispering when they rustled at night? Well, they always whispered to me about the sea. Sometimes they said names out of the geography books. In a high wind they had a desperate sound, like someone trying to tear loose."

"How funny, Nils," said Eric dreamily, resting his chin on his hand. "That tree still talks like that, and 'most always it talks to me about you."

They sat a while longer, watching the stars. At last Eric whispered anxiously: "Hadn't we better go back now? Mother will get tired waiting for us." They rose and took a short cut home, through the pasture.

II

The next morning Nils woke with the first flood of light that came with dawn. The white-plastered walls of his room reflected the glare that shone through the thin window shades, and he found it impossible to sleep. He dressed hurriedly and slipped down the hall and up the back stairs to the half-story room which he used to share with his little brother. Eric, in a skimpy nightshirt, was sitting on the edge of the bed, rubbing his eyes, his pale yellow hair standing up in tufts all over his head. When he saw Nils, he murmured something confusedly and hustled his long legs into his trousers. "I didn't expect you'd be up so early, Nils," he said, as his head emerged from his blue shirt.

"Oh, you thought I was a dude, did you?" Nils gave him a playful tap which bent the tall boy up like a clasp knife. "See here; I must teach you to box." Nils thrust his hands into his pockets and walked about. "You haven't changed things much up here. Got most of my old traps, haven't you?"

He took down a bent, withered piece of sapling that hung over the dresser. "If this isn't the stick Lou Sandberg killed himself with!"

The boy looked up from his shoe-lacing.

"Yes; you never used to let me play with that. Just how did he do it, Nils? You were with father when he found Lou, weren't you?"

"Yes. Father was going off to preach somewhere, and, as we drove along, Lou's place looked sort of forlorn, and we thought we'd stop and cheer him up. When we found him father said he'd been dead a couple days. He'd tied a piece of binding twine round his neck, made a noose in each end, fixed the nooses over the ends of a bent stick, and let the stick spring straight; strangled himself."

"What made him kill himself such a silly way?"

The simplicity of the boy's question set Nils laughing. He clapped little Eric on the shoulder. "What made him such a silly as to kill himself at all, I should say!"

"Oh, well! But his hogs had the cholera, and all up and died on him, didn't they?"

"Sure they did; but he didn't have cholera; and there were plenty of hogs left in the world, weren't there?"

"Well, but, if they weren't his, how could they do him any good?" Eric asked, in astonishment.

"Oh, scat! He could have had lots of fun with other people's hogs. He was a chump, Lou Sandberg. To kill yourself for a pig—think of that, now!" Nils laughed all the way downstairs, and quite embarrassed little Eric, who fell to scrubbing his face and hands at the tin basin. While he was parting his wet hair at the kitchen looking glass, a heavy tread sounded on the stairs. The boy dropped his comb. "Gracious, there's Mother. We must have talked too long." He hurried out to the shed, slipped on his overalls, and disappeared with the milking pails.

Mrs. Ericson came in, wearing a clean white apron, her black hair shining from the application of a wet brush.

"Good morning, Mother. Can't I make the fire for you?"

"No, thank you, Nils. It's no trouble to make a cob fire, and I like to manage the kitchen stove myself." Mrs. Ericson paused with a shovel full of ashes in her hand. "I expect you will be wanting to see your brothers as soon as possible. I'll take you up to Anders' place this morning. He's threshing, and most of our boys are over there."

"Will Olaf be there?"

Mrs. Ericson went on taking out the ashes, and spoke between shovels. "No; Olaf's wheat is all in, put away in his new barn. He got six thousand bushel this year. He's going to town today to get men to finish roofing his barn."

"So Olaf is building a new barn?" Nils asked absently.

"Biggest one in the county, and almost done. You'll likely be here for the barn-raising. He's going to have a supper and a dance as soon as everybody's done threshing. Says it keeps the voters in good humour. I tell him that's all nonsense; but Olaf has a head for politics."

"Does Olaf farm all Cousin Henrik's land?"

Mrs. Ericson frowned as she blew into the faint smoke curling up about the cobs. "Yes; he holds it in trust for the children, Hilda and her brothers. He keeps strict account of everything he raises on it, and puts the proceeds out at compound interest for them."

Nils smiled as he watched the little flames shoot up. The door of the back stairs opened, and Hilda emerged, her arms behind her, buttoning up her long gingham apron as she came. He nodded to her gaily, and she twinkled at him out of her little blue eyes, set far apart over her wide cheekbones.

"There, Hilda, you grind the coffee—and just put in an extra handful; I expect your Cousin Nils likes his strong," said Mrs. Ericson, as she went out to the shed.

Nils turned to look at the little girl, who gripped the coffee grinder between her knees and ground so hard that her two braids bobbed and her face flushed under its broad spattering of freckles. He noticed on her middle finger something that had not been there last night, and that had evidently been put on for company: a tiny gold ring with a clumsily set garnet stone. As her hand went round and round he touched the ring with the tip of his finger, smiling.

Hilda glanced toward the shed door through which Mrs. Ericson had disappeared. "My Cousin Clara gave me that," she whispered bashfully. "She's Cousin Olaf's wife."

III

Mrs. Olaf Ericson—Clara Vavrika, as many people still called her—was moving restlessly about her big bare house that morning. Her husband had left for the county town before his wife was out of bed—her lateness in rising was one of the many things the Ericson family had against her. Clara seldom came downstairs before eight o'clock, and this morning she was even later, for she had dressed with unusual care. She put on, however, only a tight-fitting black dress, which people thereabouts thought very plain. She was a tall, dark woman of thirty, with a rather sallow complexion and a touch of dull salmon red in her cheeks, where the blood seemed to burn under her brown skin. Her hair, parted evenly above her low forehead, was so black that there were distinctly blue lights in it. Her black eyebrows were delicate half-moons and her lashes were long and heavy. Her eyes slanted a little, as if she had a strain of Tartar or gypsy blood, and were sometimes full of fiery determination and sometimes dull and opaque. Her expression was never altogether amiable; was often, indeed, distinctly sullen, or, when she was animated, sarcastic. She was most attractive in profile, for then one saw to advantage her small, well-shaped head and delicate ears, and felt at once that here was a very positive, if not an altogether pleasing, personality.

The entire management of Mrs. Olaf's household devolved upon her aunt, Johanna Vavrika, a superstitious, doting woman of fifty. When Clara was a little girl her mother died, and Johanna's life had been spent in ungrudging service to her niece. Clara, like many self-willed and discontented persons, was really very apt, without knowing it, to do as other people told her, and to let her destiny be decided for her by intelligences much below her own. It was her Aunt Johanna who had humoured and spoiled her in her girlhood, who had got her off to Chicago to study piano, and who had finally persuaded her to marry

Olaf Ericson as the best match she would be likely to make in that part of the country. Johanna Vavrika had been deeply scarred by smallpox in the old country. She was short and fat, homely and jolly and sentimental. She was so broad, and took such short steps when she walked, that her brother, Joe Vavrika, always called her his duck. She adored her niece because of her talent, because of her good looks and masterful ways, but most of all because of her selfishness.

Clara's marriage with Olaf Ericson was Johanna's particular triumph. She was inordinately proud of Olaf's position, and she found a sufficiently exciting career in managing Clara's house, in keeping it above the criticism of the Ericsons, in pampering Olaf to keep him from finding fault with his wife, and in concealing from every one Clara's domestic infelicities. While Clara slept of a morning, Johanna Vavrika was bustling about, seeing that Olaf and the men had their breakfast, and that the cleaning or the butter-making or the washing was properly begun by the two girls in the kitchen. Then, at about eight o'clock, she would take Clara's coffee up to her, and chat with her while she drank it, telling her what was going on in the house. Old Mrs. Ericson frequently said that her daughter-in-law would not know what day of the week it was if Johanna did not tell her every morning. Mrs. Ericson despised and pitied Johanna, but did not wholly dislike her. The one thing she hated in her daughter-in-law above everything else was the way in which Clara could come it over people. It enraged her that the affairs of her son's big, barnlike house went on as well as they did, and she used to feel that in this world we have to wait overlong to see the guilty punished. "Suppose Johanna Vavrika died or got sick?" the old lady used to say to Olaf. "Your wife wouldn't know where to look for her own dish-cloth." Olaf only shrugged his shoulders. The fact remained that Johanna did not die, and, although Mrs. Ericson often told her she was looking poorly, she was never ill. She seldom left the house, and she slept in a little room off the kitchen. No

Ericson, by night or day, could come prying about there to find fault without her knowing it. Her one weakness was that she was an incurable talker, and she sometimes made trouble without meaning to.

This morning Clara was tying a wine-coloured ribbon about her throat when Johanna appeared with her coffee. After putting the tray on a sewing table, she began to make Clara's bed, chattering the while in Bohemian.

"Well, Olaf got off early, and the girls are baking. I'm going down presently to make some poppy-seed bread for Olaf. He asked for prune preserves at breakfast, and I told him I was out of them, and to bring some prunes and honey and cloves from town."

Clara poured her coffee. "Ugh! I don't see how men can eat so much sweet stuff. In the morning, too!"

Her aunt chuckled knowingly. "Bait a bear with honey, as we say in the old country."

"Was he cross?" her niece asked indifferently.

"Olaf? Oh, no! He was in fine spirits. He's never cross if you know how to take him. I never knew a man to make so little fuss about bills. I gave him a list of things to get a yard long, and he didn't say a word; just folded it up and put it in his pocket."

"I can well believe he didn't say a word," Clara remarked with a shrug. "Some day he'll forget how to talk."

"Oh, but they say he's a grand speaker in the Legislature. He knows when to keep quiet. That's why he's got such influence in politics. The people have confidence in him." Johanna beat up a pillow and held it under her fat chin while she slipped on the case. Her niece laughed.

"Maybe we could make people believe we were wise, Aunty, if we held our tongues. Why did you tell Mrs. Ericson that Norman threw me again last Saturday and turned my foot? She's been talking to Olaf."

Johanna fell into great confusion. "Oh, but, my precious, the old lady asked for you, and she's always so angry if I can't give an excuse.

Anyhow, she needn't talk; she's always tearing up something with that motor of hers."

When her aunt clattered down to the kitchen, Clara went to dust the parlour. Since there was not much there to dust, this did not take very long. Olaf had built the house new for her before their marriage, but her interest in furnishing it had been short-lived. It went, indeed, little beyond a bathtub and her piano. They had disagreed about almost every other article of furniture, and Clara had said she would rather have her house empty than full of things she didn't want. The house was set in a hillside, and the west windows of the parlour looked out above the kitchen yard thirty feet below. The east windows opened directly into the front yard. At one of the latter, Clara, while she was dusting, heard a low whistle. She did not turn at once, but listened intently as she drew her cloth slowly along the round of a chair. Yes, there it was:

I dreamt that I dwelt in ma-a-arble halls.

She turned and saw Nils Ericson laughing in the sunlight, his hat in his hand, just outside the window. As she crossed the room he leaned against the wire screen. "Aren't you at all surprised to see me, Clara Vavrika?"

"No; I was expecting to see you. Mother Ericson telephoned Olaf last night that you were here."

Nils squinted and gave a long whistle. "Telephoned? That must have been while Eric and I were out walking. Isn't she enterprising? Lift this screen, won't you?"

Clara lifted the screen, and Nils swung his leg across the window-sill. As he stepped into the room she said: "You didn't think you were going to get ahead of your mother, did you?"

He threw his hat on the piano. "Oh, I do sometimes. You see, I'm ahead of her now. I'm supposed to be in Anders' wheat-field. But, as we were leaving, Mother ran her car into a soft place beside the road and sank up to the hubs. While they were going for the horses to pull her out, I cut away behind the stacks and escaped." Nils chuckled. Clara's dull eyes lit up as she looked at him admiringly.

"You've got them guessing already. I don't know what your mother said to Olaf over the telephone, but he came back looking as if he'd seen a ghost, and he didn't go to bed until a dreadful hour—ten o'clock, I should think. He sat out on the porch in the dark like a graven image. It had been one of his talkative days, too." They both laughed, easily and lightly, like people who have laughed a great deal together; but they remained standing.

"Anders and Otto and Peter looked as if they had seen ghosts, too, over in the threshing field. What's the matter with them all?"

Clara gave him a quick, searching look. "Well, for one thing, they've always been afraid you have the other will."

Nils looked interested. "The other will?"

"Yes. A later one. They knew your father made another, but they never knew what he did with it. They almost tore the old house to pieces looking for it. They always suspected that he carried on a clandestine correspondence with you, for the one thing he would do was to get his own mail himself. So they thought he might have sent the new will to you for safekeeping. The old one, leaving everything to your mother, was made long before you went away, and it's understood among them that it cuts you out—that she will leave all the property to the others. Your father made the second will to prevent that. I've been hoping you had it. It would be such fun to spring it on them." Clara laughed mirthfully, a thing she did not often do now.

Nils shook his head reprovingly. "Come, now, you're malicious."

"No, I'm not. But I'd like something to happen to stir them all up, just for once. There never was such a family for having nothing ever happen to them but dinner and threshing. I'd almost be willing to die, just to have a funeral. *You* wouldn't stand it for three weeks."

Nils bent over the piano and began pecking at the keys with the finger of one hand. "I wouldn't? My dear young lady, how do you know what I can stand? *You* wouldn't wait to find out."

Clara flushed darkly and frowned. "I didn't believe you would ever come back—" she said defiantly.

"Eric believed I would, and he was only a baby when I went away. However, all's well that ends well, and I haven't come back to be a skeleton at the feast. We mustn't quarrel. Mother will be here with a search warrant pretty soon." He swung round and faced her, thrusting his hands into his coat pockets. "Come, you ought to be glad to see me, if you want something to happen. I'm something, even without a will. We can have a little fun, can't we? I think we can!"

She echoed him, "I think we can!" They both laughed and their eyes sparkled. Clara Vavrika looked ten years younger than when she had put the velvet ribbon about her throat that morning.

"You know, I'm so tickled to see mother," Nils went on. "I didn't know I was so proud of her. A regular pile driver. How about little pigtails, down at the house? Is Olaf doing the square thing by those children?"

Clara frowned pensively. "Olaf has to do something that looks like the square thing, now that he's a public man!" She glanced drolly at Nils. "But he makes a good commission out of it. On Sundays they all get together here and figure. He lets Peter and Anders put in big bills for the keep of the two boys, and he pays them out of the estate. They are always having what they call accountings. Olaf gets something out of it, too. I don't know just how they do it, but it's entirely a family matter, as they say. And when the Ericsons say that—" Clara lifted her eyebrows.

Just then the angry *honk-honk* of an approaching motor sounded from down the road. Their eyes met and they began to laugh. They laughed as children do when they can not contain themselves, and can not explain the cause of their mirth to grown people, but share it perfectly together. When Clara Vavrika sat down at the piano after he was gone, she felt that she had laughed away a dozen years. She practised as if the house were burning over her head.

When Nils greeted his mother and climbed into the front seat of the motor beside her, Mrs. Ericson looked grim, but she made no comment upon his truancy until she had turned her car and was retracing her revolutions along the road that ran by Olaf's big pasture. Then she remarked dryly:

"If I were you I wouldn't see too much of Olaf's wife while you are here. She's the kind of woman who can't see much of men without getting herself talked about. She was a good deal talked about before he married her."

"Hasn't Olaf tamed her?" Nils asked indifferently.

Mrs. Ericson shrugged her massive shoulders. "Olaf don't seem to have much luck, when it comes to wives. The first one was meek enough, but she was always ailing. And this one has her own way. He says if he quarreled with her she'd go back to her father, and then he'd lose the Bohemian vote. There are a great many Bohunks in this district. But when you find a man under his wife's thumb you can always be sure there's a soft spot in him somewhere."

Nils thought of his own father, and smiled. "She brought him a good deal of money, didn't she, besides the Bohemian vote?"

Mrs. Ericson sniffed. "Well, she has a fair half section in her own name, but I can't see as that does Olaf much good. She will have a good deal of property some day, if old Vavrika don't marry again. But I don't consider a saloonkeeper's money as good as other people's money."

Nils laughed outright. "Come, Mother, don't let your prejudices carry you that far. Money's money. Old Vavrika's a mighty decent sort of saloonkeeper. Nothing rowdy about him."

Mrs. Ericson spoke up angrily. "Oh, I know you always stood up for them! But hanging around there when you were a boy never did you any good, Nils, nor any of the other boys who went there. There weren't so many after her when she married Olaf, let me tell you. She knew enough to grab her chance."

Nils settled back in his seat. "Of course I liked to go there, Mother, and you were always cross about it. You never took the trouble to find out that it was the one jolly house in this country for a boy to go to. All the rest of you were working yourselves to death, and the houses were mostly a mess, full of babies and washing and flies. Oh, it was all right—I understand that; but you are young only once, and I happened to be young then. Now, Vavrika's was always jolly. He played the violin, and I used to take my flute, and Clara played the piano, and Johanna used to sing Bohemian songs. She always had a big supper for us—herrings and pickles and poppy-seed bread, and lots of cake and preserves. Old Joe had been in the army in the old country, and he could tell lots of good stories. I can see him cutting bread, at the head of the table, now. I don't know what I'd have done when I was a kid if it hadn't been for the Vavrikas, really."

"And all the time he was taking money that other people had worked hard in the fields for," Mrs. Ericson observed.

"So do the circuses, Mother, and they're a good thing. People ought to get fun for some of their money. Even father liked old Joe."

"Your father," Mrs. Ericson said grimly, "liked everybody."

As they crossed the sand creek and turned into her own place, Mrs. Ericson observed, "There's Olaf's buggy. He's stopped on his way from town." Nils shook himself and prepared to greet his brother, who was waiting on the porch.

Olaf was a big, heavy Norwegian, slow of speech and movement. His head was large and square, like a block of wood. When Nils, at a distance, tried to remember what his brother looked like, he could recall only his heavy head, high forehead, large nostrils, and pale blue eyes, set far apart. Olaf's features were rudimentary: the thing one noticed was the face itself, wide and flat and pale; devoid of any expression, betraying his fifty years as little as it betrayed anything else, and powerful by reason of its very stolidness. When Olaf shook hands with Nils he looked at him from under his light eyebrows, but Nils felt that no one could ever say what that pale look might mean. The one thing he had always felt in Olaf was a heavy stubbornness, like the unyielding stickiness of wet loam against the plow. He had always found Olaf the most difficult of his brothers.

"How do you do, Nils? Expect to stay with us long?"

"Oh, I may stay forever," Nils answered gaily. "I like this country better than I used to."

"There's been some work put into it since you left," Olaf remarked.

"Exactly. I think it's about ready to live in now—and I'm about ready to settle down." Nils saw his brother lower his big head ("Exactly like a bull," he thought.) "Mother's been persuading me to slow down now, and go in for farming," he went on lightly.

Olaf made a deep sound in his throat. "Farming ain't learned in a day," he brought out, still looking at the ground.

"Oh, I know! But I pick things up quickly." Nils had not meant to antagonize his brother, and he did not know now why he was doing it. "Of course," he went on, "I shouldn't expect to make a big success, as you fellows have done. But then, I'm not ambitious. I won't want much. A little land, and some cattle, maybe."

Olaf still stared at the ground, his head down. He wanted to ask Nils what he had been doing all these years, that he didn't have a business somewhere he couldn't afford to leave; why he hadn't more pride than to come back with only a little sole-leather trunk to show for himself, and to present himself as the only failure in the family. He did not ask one of these questions, but he made them all felt distinctly.

"Humph!" Nils thought. "No wonder the man never talks, when he can butt his ideas into you like that without ever saying a word. I suppose he uses that kind of smokeless powder on his wife all the time. But I guess she has her innings." He chuckled, and Olaf looked up. "Never mind me, Olaf. I laugh without knowing why, like little Eric. He's another cheerful dog."

"Eric," said Olaf slowly, "is a spoiled kid. He's just let his mother's best cow go dry because he don't milk her right. I was hoping you'd take him away somewhere and put him into business. If he don't do any good among strangers, he never will." This was a long speech for Olaf, and as he finished it he climbed into his buggy.

Nils shrugged his shoulders. "Same old tricks," he thought. "Hits from behind you every time. What a whale of a man!" He turned and went round to the kitchen, where his mother was scolding little Eric for letting the gasoline get low.

IV

Joe Vavrika's saloon was not in the county seat, where Olaf and Mrs. Ericson did their trading, but in a cheerfuller place, a little Bohemian settlement which lay at the other end of the county, ten level miles north of Olaf's farm. Clara rode up to see her father almost every day. Vavrika's house was, so to speak, in the back yard of his saloon. The garden between the two buildings was inclosed by a high board fence as tight as a partition, and in summer Joe kept beer tables and wooden benches among the gooseberry bushes under his little cherry tree. At one of these tables Nils Ericson was seated in the late afternoon, three days after his return home. Joe had gone in to serve a customer, and Nils was lounging on his elbows, looking rather mournfully into his half-emptied pitcher, when he heard a laugh across the little garden. Clara, in her riding habit, was standing at the back door of the house, under the grapevine trellis that old Joe had grown there long ago. Nils rose.

"Come out and keep your father and me company. We've been gossiping all afternoon. Nobody to bother us but the flies."

She shook her head. "No, I never come out here any more. Olaf doesn't like it. I must live up to my position, you know."

"You mean to tell me you never come out and chat with the boys, as you used to? He *has* tamed you! Who keeps up these flower-beds?"

"I come out on Sundays, when father is alone, and read the Bohemian papers to him. But I am never here when the bar is open. What have you two been doing?"

"Talking, as I told you. I've been telling him about my travels. I find I can't talk much at home, not even to Eric."

Clara reached up and poked with her riding-whip at a white moth that was fluttering in the sunlight among the vine leaves. "I suppose you will never tell me about all those things."

"Where can I tell them? Not in Olaf's house, certainly. What's the matter with our talking here?" He pointed persuasively with his hat to the bushes and the green table, where the flies were singing lazily above the empty beer glasses.

Clara shook her head weakly. "No, it wouldn't do. Besides, I am going now."

"I'm on Eric's mare. Would you be angry if I overtook you?"

Clara looked back and laughed. "You might try and see. I can leave you if I don't want you. Eric's mare can't keep up with Norman."

Nils went into the bar and attempted to pay his score. Big Joe, six feet four, with curly yellow hair and mustache, clapped him on the shoulder. "Not a Goddamn a your money go in my drawer, you hear? Only next time you bring your flute, te-te-te-te-te-ty." Joe wagged his fingers in imitation of the flute player's position. "My Clara, she come all-a-time Sundays an' play for me. She not like to play at Ericson's place." He shook his yellow curls and laughed. "Not a Goddamn a fun at Ericson's. You come a Sunday. You like-a fun. No forget de flute." Joe talked very rapidly and always tumbled over his English. He seldom spoke it to his customers, and had never learned much.

Nils swung himself into the saddle and trotted to the west of the village, where the houses and gardens scattered into prairie land and the road turned south. Far ahead of him, in the declining light, he saw Clara Vavrika's slender figure, loitering on horseback. He touched his mare with the whip, and shot along the white, level road, under the reddening sky. When he overtook Olaf's wife he saw that she had been crying. "What's the matter, Clara Vavrika?" he asked kindly.

"Oh, I get blue sometimes. It was awfully jolly living there with father. I wonder why I ever went away."

Nils spoke in a low, kind tone that he sometimes used with women: "That's what I've been wondering these many years. You were the last girl in the country I'd have picked for a wife for Olaf. What made you do it, Clara?"

"I suppose I really did it to oblige the neighbours"—Clara tossed her head. "People were beginning to wonder."

"To wonder?"

"Yes—why I didn't get married. I suppose I didn't like to keep them in suspense. I've discovered that most girls marry out of consideration for the neighbourhood."

Nils bent his head toward her and his white teeth flashed. "I'd have gambled that one girl I knew would say, 'Let the neighbourhood be damned.' "

Clara shook her head mournfully. "You see, they have it on you, Nils; that is, if you're a woman. They say you're beginning to go off. That's what makes us get married: we can't stand the laugh."

Nils looked sidewise at her. He had never seen her head droop before. Resignation was the last thing he would have expected of her. "In your case, there wasn't something else?"

"Something else?"

"I mean, you didn't do it to spite somebody? Somebody who didn't come back?"

Clara drew herself up. "Oh, I never thought you'd come back. Not after I stopped writing to you, at least. *That* was all over, long before I married Olaf."

"It never occurred to you, then, that the meanest thing you could do to me was to marry Olaf?"

Clara laughed. "No; I didn't know you were so fond of Olaf."

Nils smoothed his horse's mane with his glove. "You know, Clara Vavrika, you are never going to stick it out. You'll cut away some day, and I've been thinking you might as well cut away with me."

Clara threw up her chin. "Oh, you don't know me as well as you think. I won't cut away. Sometimes, when I'm with father, I feel like it. But I can hold out as long as the Ericsons can. They've never got the best of me yet, and one can live, so long as one isn't beaten. If I go back to father, it's all up with Olaf in politics. He knows that, and he never goes much beyond sulking. I've as much wit as the Ericsons. I'll never leave them unless I can show them a thing or two."

"You mean unless you can come it over them?"

"Yes—unless I go away with a man who is cleverer than they are, and who has more money."

Nils whistled. "Dear me, you are demanding a good deal. The Ericsons, take the lot of them, are a bunch to beat. But I should think the excitement of tormenting them would have worn off by this time."

"It has, I'm afraid," Clara admitted mournfully.

"Then why don't you cut away? There are more amusing games than this in the world. When I came home I thought it might amuse me to bully a few quarter sections out of the Ericsons; but I've almost decided I can get more fun for my money somewhere else."

Clara took in her breath sharply. "Ah, you have got the other will! That was why you came home!"

"No, it wasn't. I came home to see how you were getting on with Olaf."

Clara struck her horse with the whip, and in a bound she was far ahead of him. Nils dropped one word, "Damn!" and whipped after her; but she leaned forward in her saddle and fairly cut the wind. Her long riding skirt rippled in the still air behind her. The sun was just sinking behind the stubble in a vast, clear sky, and the shadows drew across the fields so rapidly that Nils could scarcely keep in sight the dark figure on the road. When he overtook her he caught her horse by the bridle. Norman reared, and Nils was frightened for her; but Clara kept her seat.

"Let me go, Nils Ericson!" she cried. "I hate you more than any of them. You were created to torture me, the whole tribe of you—to make me suffer in every possible way."

She struck her horse again and galloped away from him. Nils set his teeth and looked thoughtful. He rode slowly home along the deserted road, watching the stars come out in the clear violet sky. They flashed softly into the limpid heavens, like jewels let fall into clear water. They were a reproach, he felt, to a sordid world. As he turned across the sand creek, he looked up at the North Star and smiled, as if there were an understanding between them. His mother scolded him for being late for supper.

V

On Sunday afternoon Joe Vavrika, in his shirt sleeves and carpet slippers, was sitting in his garden, smoking a long-tasseled porcelain pipe with a hunting scene painted on the bowl. Clara sat under the cherry tree, reading aloud to him from the weekly Bohemian papers. She had worn a white muslin dress under her riding habit, and the leaves of the cherry tree threw a pattern of sharp shadows over her skirt. The black cat was dozing in the sunlight at her feet, and Joe's dachshund was scratching a hole under the scarlet geraniums and dreaming of badgers. Joe was filling his pipe for the third time since dinner, when he heard a knocking on the fence. He broke into a loud guffaw and unlatched the little door that led into the street. He did not call Nils by name, but caught him by the hand and dragged him in. Clara stiffened and the colour deepened under her dark skin. Nils, too, felt a little awkward. He had not seen her since the night when she rode away from him and left him alone on the level road between the fields. Joe dragged him to the wooden bench beside the green table.

"You bring de flute," he cried, tapping the leather case under Nils' arm. "Ah, das-a good! Now we have some liddle fun like old times. I got somet'ing good for you." Joe shook his finger at Nils and winked his blue eye, a bright clear eye, full of fire, though the tiny blood vessels on the ball were always a little distended. "I got somet'ing for you from"—he paused and waved his hand—"Hongarie. You know Hongarie? You wait!" He pushed Nils down on the bench, and went through the back door of his saloon.

Nils looked at Clara, who sat frigidly with her white skirts drawn tight about her. "He didn't tell you he had asked me to come, did he? He wanted a party and proceeded to arrange it. Isn't he fun? Don't be cross; let's give him a good time."

Clara smiled and shook out her skirt. "Isn't that like father? And he has sat here so meekly all day. Well, I won't pout. I'm glad you came. He doesn't have very many good times now any more. There are so few of his kind left. The second generation are a tame lot."

Joe came back with a flask in one hand and three wine glasses caught by the stems between the fingers of the other. These he placed on the table with an air of ceremony, and, going behind Nils, held the flask between him and the sun, squinting into it admiringly. "You know dis, Tokai? A great friend of mine, he bring dis to me, a present out of Hongarie. You know how much it cost, dis wine? Chust so much what it weigh in gold. Nobody but de nobles drink him in Bohemie. Many, many years I save him up, dis Tokai." Joe whipped out his official corkscrew and delicately removed the cork. "De old man die what bring him to me, an' dis wine he lay on his belly in my cellar an' sleep. An' now," carefully pouring out the heavy yellow wine, "an' now he wake up; and maybe he wake us up, too!" He carried one of the glasses to his daughter and presented it with great gallantry.

Clara shook her head, but, seeing her father's disappointment, relented. "You taste it first. I don't want so much."

Joe sampled it with a beatific expression, and turned to Nils. "You drink him slow, dis wine. He very soft, but he go down hot. You see!"

After a second glass Nils declared that he couldn't take any more without getting sleepy. "Now get your fiddle, Vavrika," he said as he opened his flute case.

But Joe settled back in his wooden rocker and wagged his big carpet slipper. "No-no-no-no-no-no-no! No play fiddle now any more: too much ache in de finger," waving them, "all-a-time rheumatiz. You play de flute, te-tety-te-tety-te. Bohemie songs."

"I've forgotten all the Bohemian songs I used to play with you and Johanna. But here's one that will make Clara pout. You remember how her eyes used to snap when we called her the Bohemian Girl?" Nils lifted his flute and began "When Other Lips and Other Hearts," and Joe hummed the air in a husky baritone, waving his carpet slipper. "Oh-h-h, das-a fine music," he cried, clapping his hands as Nils finished. "Now 'Marble Halls, Marble Halls'! Clara, you sing him."

Clara smiled and leaned back in her chair, beginning softly:

"I dreamt that I dwelt in ma-a-arble halls,
With vassals and serfs at my knee,"

and Joe hummed like a big bumblebee.

"There's one more you always played," Clara said quietly, "I remember that best." She locked her hands over her knee and began "The Heart Bowed Down," and sang it through without groping for the words. She was singing with a good deal of warmth when she came to the end of the old song:

"For memory is the only friend
That grief can call its own."

Joe flashed out his red silk handkerchief and blew his nose, shaking his head. "No-no-no-no-no-no-no! Too sad, too sad! I not like-a dat. Play quick somet'ing gay now."

Nils put his lips to the instrument, and Joe lay back in his chair, laughing and singing, "Oh, Evelina, Sweet Evelina!" Clara laughed, too. Long ago, when she and Nils went to high school, the model student of their class was a very homely girl in thick spectacles. Her name was Evelina Oleson; she had a long, swinging walk which somehow suggested the measure of that song, and they used mercilessly to sing it at her.

"Dat ugly Oleson girl, she teach in de school," Joe gasped, "an' she still walks chust like dat, yup-a, yup-a, yup-a, chust like a camel she go! Now, Nils, we have some more li'l drink. Oh, yes-yes-yes-yes-yes-yes-*yes*! Dis time you haf to drink, and Clara she haf to, so she show she not jealous. So, we all drink to your girl. You not tell her name, eh? No-no-no, I no make you tell. She pretty, eh? She make good sweetheart? I bet!" Joe winked and lifted his glass. "How soon you get married?"

Nils screwed up his eyes. "That I don't know. When she says."

Joe threw out his chest. "Das-a way boys talks. No way for mans. Mans say, 'You come to de church, an' get a hurry on you.' Das-a way mans talks."

"Maybe Nils hasn't got enough to keep a wife," put in Clara ironically. "How about that, Nils?" she asked him frankly, as if she wanted to know.

Nils looked at her coolly, raising one eyebrow. "Oh, I can keep her, all right."

"The way she wants to be kept?"

"With my wife, I'll decide that," replied Nils calmly. "I'll give her what's good for her."

Clara made a wry face. "You'll give her the strap, I expect, like old Peter Oleson gave his wife."

"When she needs it," said Nils lazily, locking his hands behind his head and squinting up through the leaves of the cherry tree. "Do you remember the time I squeezed the cherries all over your clean dress, and Aunt Johanna boxed my ears for me? My gracious, weren't you mad! You had both hands full of cherries, and I squeezed 'em and made the juice fly all over you. I liked to have fun with you; you'd get so mad."

"We *did* have fun, didn't we? None of the other kids ever had so much fun. We knew how to play."

Nils dropped his elbows on the table and looked steadily across at her. "I've played with lots of girls since, but I haven't found one who was such good fun."

Clara laughed. The late afternoon sun was shining full in her face, and deep in the back of her eyes there shone something fiery, like the yellow drops of Tokai in the brown glass bottle. "Can you still play, or are you only pretending?"

"I can play better than I used to, and harder."

"Don't you ever work, then?" She had not intended to say it. It slipped out because she was confused enough to say just the wrong thing.

"I work between times." Nils' steady gaze still beat upon her. "Don't you worry about my working, Mrs. Ericson. You're getting like all the rest of them." He reached his brown, warm hand across the table and dropped it on Clara's, which was cold as an icicle. "Last call for play, Mrs. Ericson!" Clara shivered, and suddenly her hands and cheeks grew warm. Her fingers lingered in his a moment, and they looked at each other earnestly. Joe Vavrika had put the mouth of the bottle to his lips and was swallowing the last drops of the Tokai, standing. The sun, just about to sink behind his shop, glistened on the bright glass, on his flushed face and curly yellow hair. "Look," Clara whispered, "that's the way I want to grow old."

VI

On the day of Olaf Ericson's barn-raising, his wife, for once in a way, rose early. Johanna Vavrika had been baking cakes and frying and boiling and spicing meats for a week beforehand, but it was not until the day before the party was to take place that Clara showed any interest in it. Then she was seized with one of her fitful spasms of energy, and took the wagon and little Eric and spent the day on Plum Creek, gathering vines and swamp goldenrod to decorate the barn.

By four o'clock in the afternoon buggies and wagons began to arrive at the big unpainted building in front of Olaf's house. When Nils and his mother came at five, there were more than fifty people in the barn, and a great drove of children. On the ground floor stood six long tables, set with the crockery of seven flourishing Ericson families, lent for the occasion. In the middle of each table was a big yellow pumpkin, hollowed out and filled with woodbine. In one corner of the barn, behind a pile of green-and-white striped watermelons, was a circle of chairs for the old people; the younger guests sat on bushel measures or barbed-wire spools, and the children tumbled about in the haymow. The box stalls Clara had converted into booths. The framework was hidden by goldenrod and sheaves of wheat, and the partitions were covered with wild grapevines full of fruit. At one of these Johanna Vavrika watched over her cooked meats, enough to provision an army; and at the next her kitchen girls had ranged the ice-cream freezers, and Clara was already cutting pies and cakes against the hour of serving. At the third stall, little Hilda, in a bright pink lawn dress, dispensed lemonade throughout the afternoon. Olaf, as a public man, had thought it inadvisable to serve beer in his barn; but Joe Vavrika had come over with two demijohns concealed in his buggy, and after his arrival the wagon shed was much frequented by the men.

"Hasn't Cousin Clara fixed things lovely?" little Hilda whispered, when Nils went up to her stall and asked for lemonade.

Nils leaned against the booth, talking to the excited little girl and watching the people. The barn faced the west, and the sun, pouring in at the big doors, filled the whole interior with a golden light, through which filtered fine particles of dust from the haymow, where the children were romping. There was a great chattering from the stall where Johanna Vavrika exhibited to the admiring women her platters heaped with fried chicken, her roasts of beef, boiled tongues, and baked hams with cloves stuck in the crisp brown fat and garnished with tansy and parsley. The older women, having assured themselves that there were twenty kinds of cake, not counting cookies, and three dozen fat pies, repaired to the corner behind the pile of watermelons, put on their white aprons, and fell to their knitting and fancywork. They were a fine company of old women, and a Dutch painter would have loved to find them there together, where the sun made bright patches on the floor and sent long, quivering shafts of gold through the dusky shade up among the rafters. There were fat, rosy old women who looked hot in their best black dresses; spare, alert old women with brown, dark-veined hands; and several of almost heroic frame, not less massive than old Mrs. Ericson herself. Few of them wore glasses, and old Mrs. Svendsen, a Danish woman, who was quite bald, wore the only cap among them. Mrs. Oleson, who had twelve big grandchildren, could still show two braids of yellow hair as thick as her own wrists. Among all these grandmothers there were more brown heads than white. They all had a pleased, prosperous air, as if they were more than satisfied with themselves and with life. Nils, leaning against Hilda's lemonade stand, watched them as they sat chattering in four languages, their fingers never lagging behind their tongues.

"Look at them over there," he whispered, detaining Clara as she passed him. "Aren't they the Old Guard? I've just counted thirty hands. I guess they've wrung many a chicken's neck and warmed many a boy's jacket for him in their time."

In reality he fell into amazement when he thought of the Herculean labours those fifteen pairs of hands had performed: of the cows they had milked, the butter they had made, the gardens they had planted, the children and grandchildren they had tended, the brooms they had worn out, the mountains of food they had cooked. It made him dizzy. Clara Vavrika smiled a hard, enigmatical smile at him and walked rapidly away. Nils' eyes followed her white figure as she went toward the house. He watched her walking alone in the sunlight, looked at her slender, defiant shoulders and her little hard-set head with its coils of blue-black hair. "No," he reflected; "she'd never be like them, not if she lived here a hundred years. She'd only grow more bitter. You can't tame a wild thing; you can only chain it. People aren't all alike. I mustn't lose my nerve." He gave Hilda's pigtail a parting tweak and set out after Clara. "Where to?" he asked, as he came upon her in the kitchen.

"I'm going to the cellar for preserves."

"Let me go with you. I never get a moment alone with you. Why do you keep out of my way?"

Clara laughed. "I don't usually get in anybody's way."

Nils followed her down the stairs and to the far corner of the cellar, where a basement window let in a stream of light. From a swinging shelf Clara selected several glass jars, each labeled in Johanna's careful hand. Nils took up a brown flask. "What's this? It looks good."

"It is. It's some French brandy father gave me when I was married. Would you like some? Have you a corkscrew? I'll get glasses."

When she brought them, Nils took them from her and put them down on the window-sill. "Clara Vavrika, do you remember how crazy I used to be about you?"

Clara shrugged her shoulders. "Boys are always crazy about somebody or another. I dare say some silly has been crazy about Evelina Oleson. You got over it in a hurry."

"Because I didn't come back, you mean? I had to get on, you know, and it was hard sledding at first. Then I heard you'd married Olaf."

"And then you stayed away from a broken heart," Clara laughed.

"And then I began to think about you more than I had since I first went away. I began to wonder if you were really as you had seemed to me when I was a boy. I thought I'd like to see. I've had lots of girls, but no one ever pulled me the same way. The more I thought about you, the more I remembered how it used to be—like hearing a wild tune you can't resist, calling you out at night. It had been a long while since anything had pulled me out of my boots, and I wondered whether anything ever could again." Nils thrust his hands into his coat pockets and squared his shoulders, as his mother sometimes squared hers, as Olaf, in a clumsier manner, squared his. "So I thought I'd come back and see. Of course the family have tried to do me, and I rather thought I'd bring out father's will and make a fuss. But they can have their old land; they've put enough sweat into it." He took the flask and filled the two glasses carefully to the brim. "I've found out what I want from the Ericsons. Drink *skoal,* Clara." He lifted his glass, and Clara took hers with downcast eyes. "Look at me, Clara Vavrika. *Skoal!*"

She raised her burning eyes and answered fiercely: "*Skoal!*"

—

The barn supper began at six o'clock and lasted for two hilarious hours. Yense Nelson had made a wager that he could eat two whole fried chickens, and he did. Eli Swanson stowed away two whole custard pies, and Nick Hermanson ate a chocolate layer cake to the last crumb. There was even a cooky contest among the children, and one thin, slablike Bohemian boy consumed sixteen and won the prize, a gingerbread pig which Johanna Vavrika had carefully decorated with red candies and burnt sugar. Fritz Sweiheart, the German carpenter, won in the pickle contest, but he disappeared soon after supper and was not seen for the rest of the evening. Joe Vavrika said that Fritz could have managed the pickles all right, but he had sampled the demijohn in his buggy too often before sitting down to the table.

While the supper was being cleared away the two fiddlers began to tune up for the dance. Clara was to accompany them on her old upright piano, which had been brought down from her father's. By this time Nils had renewed old acquaintances. Since his interview with Clara in the cellar, he had been busy telling all the old women how young they looked, and all the young ones how pretty they were, and assuring the men that they had here the best farmland in the world. He had made himself so agreeable that old Mrs. Ericson's friends began to come up to her and tell how lucky she was to get her smart son back again, and please to get him to play his flute. Joe Vavrika, who could still play very well when he forgot that he had rheumatism, caught up a fiddle from Johnny Oleson and played a crazy Bohemian dance tune that set the wheels going. When he dropped the bow every one was ready to dance.

Olaf, in a frock coat and a solemn made-up necktie, led the grand march with his mother. Clara had kept well out of *that* by sticking to the piano. She played the march with a pompous solemnity which greatly amused the prodigal son, who went over and stood behind her.

"Oh, aren't you rubbing it into them, Clara Vavrika? And aren't you lucky to have me here, or all your wit would be thrown away."

"I'm used to being witty for myself. It saves my life."

The fiddles struck up a polka, and Nils convulsed Joe Vavrika by leading out Evelina Oleson, the homely schoolteacher. His next partner was a very fat Swedish girl, who, although she was an heiress, had not been asked for the first dance, but had stood against the wall in her tight, high-heeled shoes, nervously fingering a lace handkerchief. She was soon out of breath, so Nils led her, pleased and panting, to her seat, and went over to the piano, from which Clara had been watching his gallantry. "Ask Olena Yenson," she whispered. "She waltzes beautifully."

Olena, too, was rather inconveniently plump, handsome in a smooth, heavy way, with a fine colour and good-natured, sleepy eyes. She was redolent of violet sachet powder, and had warm, soft, white hands, but she danced divinely, moving as smoothly as the tide coming in. "There, that's something like," Nils said as he released her. "You'll give me the next waltz, won't you? Now I must go and dance with my little cousin."

Hilda was greatly excited when Nils went up to her stall and held out his arm. Her little eyes sparkled, but she declared that she could not leave her lemonade. Old Mrs. Ericson, who happened along at this moment, said she would attend to that, and Hilda came out, as pink as her pink dress. The dance was a schottische, and in a moment her yellow braids were fairly standing on end. "Bravo!" Nils cried encouragingly. "Where did you learn to dance so nicely?"

"My Cousin Clara taught me," the little girl panted.

Nils found Eric sitting with a group of boys who were too awkward or too shy to dance, and told him that he must dance the next waltz with Hilda.

The boy screwed up his shoulders. "Aw, Nils, I can't dance. My feet are too big; I look silly."

"Don't be thinking about yourself. It doesn't matter how boys look."

Nils had never spoken to him so sharply before, and Eric made haste to scramble out of his corner and brush the straw from his coat.

Clara nodded approvingly. "Good for you, Nils. I've been trying to get hold of him. They dance very nicely together; I sometimes play for them."

"I'm obliged to you for teaching him. There's no reason why he should grow up to be a lout."

"He'll never be that. He's more like you than any of them. Only he hasn't your courage." From her slanting eyes Clara shot forth one of those keen glances, admiring and at the same time challenging, which she seldom bestowed on any one, and which seemed to say, "Yes, I admire you, but I am your equal."

Clara was proving a much better host than Olaf, who, once the supper was over, seemed to feel no interest in anything but the lanterns. He had brought a locomotive headlight from town to light the revels, and he kept skulking about as if he feared the mere light from it might set his new barn on fire. His wife, on the contrary, was cordial to every one, was animated and even gay. The deep salmon colour in her cheeks burned vividly, and her eyes were full of life. She gave the piano over to the fat Swedish heiress, pulled her father away from the corner where he sat gossiping with his cronies, and made him dance a Bohemian dance with her. In his youth Joe had been a famous dancer, and his daughter got him so limbered up that every one sat around and applauded them. The old ladies were particularly delighted, and made them go through the dance again. From their corner where they watched and commented, the old women kept time with their feet and hands, and whenever the fiddles struck up a new air old Mrs. Svendsen's white cap would begin to bob.

Clara was waltzing with little Eric when Nils came up to them, brushed his brother aside, and swung her out among the dancers. "Remember how we used to waltz on rollers at the old skating rink in town? I suppose people don't do that any more. We used to keep it up for hours. You know, we never did moon around as other boys and girls did. It was dead serious with us from the beginning. When we were most in love with each other, we used to fight. You were always pinching people; your fingers were like little nippers. A regular snapping turtle, you were. Lord, how you'd like Stockholm! Sit out in the streets in front of cafés and talk all night in summer. Just like a reception—officers and ladies and funny English people. Jolliest people in the world, the Swedes, once you get them going. Always drinking things—champagne and stout mixed, half-and-half; serve it out of big pitchers, and serve plenty. Slow pulse, you know; they can stand a lot. Once they light up, they're glow-worms, I can tell you."

"All the same, you don't really like gay people."

"*I* don't?"

"No; I could tell that when you were looking at the old women there this afternoon. They're the kind you really admire, after all; women like your mother. And that's the kind you'll marry."

"Is it, Miss Wisdom? You'll see who I'll marry, and she won't have a domestic virtue to bless herself with. She'll be a snapping turtle, and she'll be a match for me. All the same, they're a fine bunch of old dames over there. You admire them yourself."

"No, I don't; I detest them."

"You won't, when you look back on them from Stockholm or Budapest. Freedom settles all that. Oh, but you're the real Bohemian Girl,

Clara Vavrika!" Nils laughed down at her sullen frown and began mockingly to sing:

> *"Oh, how could a poor gypsy maiden like me*
> *Expect the proud bride of a baron to be?"*

Clara clutched his shoulder. "Hush, Nils; every one is looking at you."

"I don't care. They can't gossip. It's all in the family, as the Ericsons say when they divide up little Hilda's patrimony amongst them. Besides, we'll give them something to talk about when we hit the trail. Lord, it will be a godsend to them! They haven't had anything so interesting to chatter about since the grasshopper year. It'll give them a new lease of life. And Olaf won't lose the Bohemian vote, either. They'll have the laugh on him so that they'll vote two apiece. They'll send him to Congress. They'll never forget his barn party, or us. They'll always remember us as we're dancing together now. We're making a legend. Where's my waltz, boys?" he called as they whirled past the fiddlers.

The musicians grinned, looked at each other, hesitated, and began a new air; and Nils sang with them, as the couples fell from a quick waltz to a long, slow glide:

> *"When other lips and other hearts*
> *Their tale of love shall tell,*
> *In language whose excess imparts*
> *The power they feel so well."*

The old women applauded vigorously. "What a gay one he is, that Nils!" And old Mrs. Svendsen's cap lurched dreamily from side to side to the flowing measure of the dance.

"Of days that have as ha-a-p-py been,
And you'll remember me."

VII

The moonlight flooded that great, silent land. The reaped fields lay yellow in it. The straw stacks and poplar windbreaks threw sharp black shadows. The roads were white rivers of dust. The sky was a deep, crystalline blue, and the stars were few and faint. Everything seemed to have succumbed, to have sunk to sleep, under the great, golden, tender, midsummer moon. The splendour of it seemed to transcend human life and human fate. The senses were too feeble to take it in, and every time one looked up at the sky one felt unequal to it, as if one were sitting deaf under the waves of a great river of melody. Near the road, Nils Ericson was lying against a straw stack in Olaf's wheat-field. His own life seemed strange and unfamiliar to him, as if it were something he had read about, or dreamed, and forgotten. He lay very still, watching the white road that ran in front of him, lost itself among the fields, and then, at a distance, reappeared over a little hill. At last, against this white band he saw something moving rapidly, and he got up and walked to the edge of the field. "She is passing the row of poplars now," he thought. He heard the padded beat of hoofs along the dusty road, and as she came into sight he stepped out and waved his arms. Then, for fear of frightening the horse, he drew back and waited. Clara had seen him, and she came up at a walk. Nils took the horse by the bit and stroked his neck.

"What are you doing out so late, Clara Vavrika? I went to the house, but Johanna told me you had gone to your father's."

"Who can stay in the house on a night like this? Aren't you out yourself?"

"Ah, but that's another matter."

Nils turned the horse into the field.

"What are you doing? Where are you taking Norman?"

"Not far, but I want to talk to you tonight; I have something to say to you. I can't talk to you at the house, with Olaf sitting there on the porch, weighing a thousand tons."

Clara laughed. "He won't be sitting there now. He's in bed by this time, and asleep—weighing a thousand tons."

Nils plodded on across the stubble. "Are you really going to spend the rest of your life like this, night after night, summer after summer? Haven't you anything better to do on a night like this than to wear yourself and Norman out tearing across the country to your father's and back? Besides, your father won't live forever, you know. His little place will be shut up or sold, and then you'll have nobody but the Ericsons. You'll have to fasten down the hatches for the winter then."

Clara moved her head restlessly. "Don't talk about that. I try never to think of it. If I lost father I'd lose everything, even my hold over the Ericsons."

"Bah! You'd lose a good deal more than that. You'd lose your race, everything that makes you yourself. You've lost a good deal of it now."

"Of what?"

"Of your love of life, your capacity for delight."

Clara put her hands up to her face. "I haven't, Nils Ericson, I haven't! Say anything to me but that. I won't have it!" she declared vehemently.

Nils led the horse up to a straw stack, and turned to Clara, looking at her intently, as he had looked at her that Sunday afternoon at Vavrika's. "But why do you fight for that so? What good is the power to enjoy, if you never enjoy? Your hands are cold again; what are you afraid of all the time? Ah, you're afraid of losing it; that's what's the matter with you! And you will, Clara Vavrika, you will! When I used to know you—listen; you've caught a wild bird in your hand, haven't you, and felt its heart beat so hard that you were afraid it would shatter its little body to pieces? Well, you used to be just like that, a slender, eager thing with a wild delight inside you. That is how I remembered you. And I come back and find you—a bitter woman. This is a perfect ferret fight here; you live by biting and being bitten. Can't you remember what life used to be? Can't you remember that old delight? I've never forgotten it, or known its like, on land or sea."

He drew the horse under the shadow of the straw stack. Clara felt him take her foot out of the stirrup, and she slid softly down into his arms. He kissed her slowly. He was a deliberate man, but his nerves were steel when he wanted anything. Something flashed out from him like a knife out of a sheath. Clara felt everything slipping away from her; she was flooded by the summer night. He thrust his hand into his pocket, and then held it out at arm's length. "Look," he said. The shadow of the straw stack fell sharp across his wrist, and in the palm of his hand she saw a silver dollar shining. "That's my pile," he muttered; "will you go with me?"

Clara nodded, and dropped her forehead on his shoulder.

Nils took a deep breath. "Will you go with me tonight?"

"Where?" she whispered softly.

"To town, to catch the midnight flyer."

Clara lifted her head and pulled herself together. "Are you crazy, Nils? We couldn't go away like that."

"That's the only way we ever will go. You can't sit on the bank and think about it. You have to plunge. That's the way I've always done, and it's the right way for people like you and me. There's nothing so dangerous as sitting still. You've only got one life, one youth, and you can let it slip through your fingers if you want to; nothing easier. Most people do that. You'd be better off tramping the roads with me than you are here." Nils held back her head and looked into her eyes. "But I'm not that kind of a tramp, Clara. You won't have to take in sewing.

I'm with a Norwegian shipping line; came over on business with the New York offices, but now I'm going straight back to Bergen. I expect I've got as much money as the Ericsons. Father sent me a little to get started. They never knew about that. There, I hadn't meant to tell you; I wanted you to come on your own nerve."

Clara looked off across the fields. "It isn't that, Nils, but something seems to hold me. I'm afraid to pull against it. It comes out of the ground, I think."

"I know all about that. One has to tear loose. You're not needed here. Your father will understand; he's made like us. As for Olaf, Johanna will take better care of him than ever you could. It's now or never, Clara Vavrika. My bag's at the station; I smuggled it there yesterday."

Clara clung to him and hid her face against his shoulder. "Not tonight," she whispered. "Sit here and talk to me tonight. I don't want to go anywhere tonight. I may never love you like this again."

Nils laughed through his teeth. "You can't come that on me. That's not my way, Clara Vavrika. Eric's mare is over there behind the stacks, and I'm off on the midnight. It's goodbye, or off across the world with me. My carriage won't wait. I've written a letter to Olaf; I'll mail it in town. When he reads it he won't bother us—not if I know him. He'd rather have the land. Besides, I could demand an investigation of his administration of Cousin Henrik's estate, and that would be bad for a public man. You've no clothes, I know; but you can sit up tonight, and we can get everything on the way. Where's your old dash, Clara Vavrika? What's become of your Bohemian blood? I used to think you had courage enough for anything. Where's your nerve—what are you waiting for?"

Clara drew back her head, and he saw the slumberous fire in her eyes. "For you to say one thing, Nils Ericson."

"I never say that thing to any woman, Clara Vavrika." He leaned back, lifted her gently from the ground, and whispered through his teeth: "But I'll never, never let you go, not to any man on earth but me! Do you understand me? Now, wait here."

Clara sank down on a sheaf of wheat and covered her face with her hands. She did not know what she was going to do—whether she would go or stay. The great, silent country seemed to lay a spell upon her. The ground seemed to hold her as if by roots. Her knees were soft under her. She felt as if she could not bear separation from her old sorrows, from her old discontent. They were dear to her, they had kept her alive, they were a part of her. There would be nothing left of her if she were wrenched away from them. Never could she pass beyond that skyline against which her restlessness had beat so many times. She felt as if her soul had built itself a nest there on that horizon at which she looked every morning and every evening, and it was dear to her, inexpressibly dear. She pressed her fingers against her eyeballs to shut it out. Beside her she heard the tramping of horses in the soft earth. Nils said nothing to her. He put his hands under her arms and lifted her lightly to her saddle. Then he swung himself into his own.

"We shall have to ride fast to catch the midnight train. A last gallop, Clara Vavrika. Forward!"

There was a start, a thud of hoofs along the moonlit road, two dark shadows going over the hill; and then the great, still land stretched untroubled under the azure night. Two shadows had passed.

VII

A year after the flight of Olaf Ericson's wife, the night train was steaming across the plains of Iowa. The conductor was hurrying through one of the day coaches, his lantern on his arm, when a lank, fair-haired boy sat up in one of the plush seats and tweaked him by the coat.

"What is the next step, please, sir?"

"Red Oak, Iowa. But you go through to Chicago, don't you?" He looked down, and noticed that the boy's eyes were red and his face was drawn, as if he were in trouble.

"Yes. But I was wondering whether I could get off at the next place and get a train back to Omaha."

"Well, I suppose you could. Live in Omaha?"

"No. In the western part of the State. How soon do we get to Red Oak?"

"Forty minutes. You'd better make up your mind, so I can tell the baggageman to put your trunk off."

"Oh, never mind about that! I mean, I haven't got any," the boy added, blushing.

"Run away," the conductor thought, as he slammed the coach door behind him.

Eric Ericson crumpled down in his seat and put his brown hand to his forehead. He had been crying, and he had had no supper, and his head was aching violently. "Oh, what shall I do?" he thought, as he looked dully down at his big shoes. "Nils will be ashamed of me; I haven't got any spunk."

Ever since Nils had run away with his brother's wife, life at home had been hard for little Eric. His mother and Olaf both suspected him of complicity. Mrs. Ericson was harsh and faultfinding, constantly wounding the boy's pride; and Olaf was always setting her against him.

Joe Vavrika heard often from his daughter. Clara had always been fond of her father, and happiness made her kinder. She wrote him long accounts of the voyage to Bergen, and of the trip she and Nils took through Bohemia to the little town where her father had grown up and where she herself was born. She visited all her kinsmen there, and sent her father news of his brother, who was a priest; of his sister, who had married a horse-breeder—of their big farm and their many children. These letters Joe always managed to read to little Eric. They contained messages for Eric and Hilda. Clara sent presents, too, which Eric never dared to take home and which poor little Hilda never even saw, though she loved to hear Eric tell about them when they were out getting the eggs together. But Olaf once saw Eric coming out of Vavrika's house—the old man had never asked the boy to come into his saloon—and Olaf went straight to his mother and told her. That night Mrs. Ericson came to Eric's room after he was in bed and made a terrible scene. She could be very terrifying when she was really angry. She forbade him ever to speak to Vavrika again, and after that night she would not allow him to go to town alone. So it was a long while before Eric got any more news of his brother. But old Joe suspected what was going on, and he carried Clara's letters about in his pocket. One Sunday he drove out to see a German friend of his, and chanced to catch sight of Eric, sitting by the cattle pond in the big pasture. They went together into Fritz Oberlies' barn, and read the letters and talked things over. Eric admitted that things were getting hard for him at home. That very night old Joe sat down and laboriously penned a statement of the case to his daughter.

Things got no better for Eric. His mother and Olaf felt that, however closely he was watched, he still, as they said, "heard." Mrs. Ericson could not admit neutrality. She had sent Johanna Vavrika packing back to her brother's, though Olaf would much rather have kept her than Anders' eldest daughter, whom Mrs. Ericson installed in her place. He was not so highhanded as his mother, and he once sulkily told her that she might better have taught her granddaughter to cook before she sent Johanna away. Olaf could have borne a good deal for the sake of prunes spiced in honey, the secret of which Johanna had taken away with her.

At last two letters came to Joe Vavrika: one from Nils, inclosing a postal order for money to pay Eric's passage to Bergen, and one from Clara, saying that Nils had a place for Eric in the offices of his company, that he was to live with them, and that they were only waiting for him to come. He was to leave New York on one of the boats of Nils' own line; the captain was one of their friends, and Eric was to make himself known at once.

Nils' directions were so explicit that a baby could have followed them, Eric felt. And here he was, nearing Red Oak, Iowa, and rocking backward and forward in despair. Never had he loved his brother so much, and never had the big world called to him so hard. But there was a lump in his throat which would not go down. Ever since nightfall he had been tormented by the thought of his mother, alone in that big house that had sent forth so many men. Her unkindness now seemed so little, and her loneliness so great. He remembered everything she had ever done for him: how frightened she had been when he tore his hand in the corn-sheller, and how she wouldn't let Olaf scold him. When Nils went away he didn't leave his mother all alone, or he would never have gone. Eric felt sure of that.

The train whistled. The conductor came in, smiling not unkindly. "Well, young man, what are you going to do? We stop at Red Oak in three minutes."

"Yes, thank you. I'll let you know." The conductor went out, and the boy doubled up with misery. He couldn't let his one chance go like this. He felt for his breast pocket and crackled Nils' letter to give him courage. He didn't want Nils to be ashamed of him. The train stopped. Suddenly he remembered his brother's kind, twinkling eyes, that always looked at you as if from far away. The lump in his throat softened. "Ah, but Nils, Nils would *understand*!" he thought. "That's just it about Nils; he always understands."

A lank, pale boy with a canvas telescope stumbled off the train to the Red Oak siding, just as the conductor called, "All aboard!"

—

The next night Mrs. Ericson was sitting alone in her wooden rocking-chair on the front porch. Little Hilda had been sent to bed and had cried herself to sleep. The old woman's knitting was on her lap, but her hands lay motionless on top of it. For more than an hour she had not moved a muscle. She simply sat, as only the Ericsons and the mountains can sit. The house was dark, and there was no sound but the croaking of the frogs down in the pond of the little pasture.

Eric did not come home by the road, but across the fields, where no one could see him. He set his telescope down softly in the kitchen shed, and slipped noiselessly along the path to the front porch. He sat down on the step without saying anything. Mrs. Ericson made no sign, and the frogs croaked on. At last the boy spoke timidly.

"I've come back, Mother."

"Very well," said Mrs. Ericson.

Eric leaned over and picked up a little stick out of the grass.

"How about the milking?" he faltered.

"That's been done, hours ago."

"Who did you get?"

"Get? I did it myself. I can milk as good as any of you."

Eric slid along the step nearer to her. "Oh, Mother, why did you?" he asked sorrowfully. "Why didn't you get one of Otto's boys?"

"I didn't want anybody to know I was in need of a boy," said Mrs. Ericson bitterly. She looked straight in front of her and her mouth tightened. "I always meant to give you the home farm," she added.

The boy stared and slid closer. "Oh, Mother," he faltered, "I don't care about the farm. I came back because I thought you might be needing me, maybe." He hung his head and got no further.

"Very well," said Mrs. Ericson. Her hand went out from her suddenly and rested on his head. Her fingers twined themselves in his soft, pale hair. His tears splashed down on the boards; happiness filled his heart.

FROM

The Tenant of Wildfell Hall

Anne Brontë

Two days after, Mrs. Graham called at Linden-Car, contrary to the expectation of Rose, who entertained an idea that the mysterious occupant of Wildfell Hall would wholly disregard the common observances of civilized life—in which opinion she was supported by the Wilsons, who testified that neither their call nor the Millwards' had been returned as yet. Now, however, the cause of that omission was explained, though not entirely to the satisfaction of Rose. Mrs. Graham had brought her child with her, and on my mother's expressing surprise that he could walk so far, she replied:

"It is a long walk for him; but I must have either taken him with me, or relinquished the visit altogether—for I never leave him alone—and I think, Mrs. Markham, I must beg you to make my excuses to the Millwards and Mrs. Wilson, when you see them, as I fear I cannot do myself the pleasure of calling upon them till my little Arthur is able to accompany me."

"But you have a servant," said Rose; "could you not leave him with her?"

"She has her own occupations to attend to; and besides, she is too old to run after a child, and he is too mercurial to be tied to an elderly woman."

"But you left him to come to church."

"Yes, once; but I would not have left him for any other purpose; and I think, in future, I must contrive to bring him with me, or stay at home."

"Is he so mischievous?" asked my mother, considerably shocked.

"No," replied the lady, sadly smiling, as she stroked the wavy locks of her son, who was seated on a low stool at her feet, "but he is my only treasure, and I am his only friend, so we don't like to be separated."

"But, my dear, I call that doting," said my plain-spoken parent. "You should try to suppress such foolish fondness, as well to save your son from ruin as yourself from ridicule."

"Ruin! Mrs. Markham?"

"Yes; it is spoiling the child. Even at his age, he ought not to be always tied to his mother's apron-string; he should learn to be ashamed of it."

"Mrs. Markham, I beg you will not say such things in his presence, at least. I trust my son will never be ashamed to love his mother!" said Mrs. Graham, with a serious energy that startled the company.

My mother attempted to appease her by an explanation; but she seemed to think enough had been said on the subject, and abruptly turned the conversation.

"Just as I thought," said I to myself: "the lady's temper is none of the mildest, notwithstanding her sweet, pale face and lofty brow, where thought and suffering seem equally to have stamped their impress."

All this time, I was seated at a table on the other side of the room, apparently immersed in the perusal of a volume of the *Farmer's Magazine,* which I happened to have been reading at the moment of our visitor's arrival; and, not choosing to be over civil, I had merely bowed as she entered, and continued my occupation as before.

In a little while, however, I was sensible that someone was approaching me, with a light, but slow and hesitating tread. It was little Arthur, irresistibly attracted by my dog Sancho, that was lying at my feet. On looking up, I beheld him standing about two yards off, with his clear blue eyes wistfully gazing on the dog, transfixed to the spot, not by fear of the animal but by a timid disinclination to approach its master. A little encouragement, however, induced him to come forward. The child, though shy, was not sullen. In a minute he was kneeling on the carpet, with his arms round Sancho's neck, and in a minute or two more the little fellow was seated on my knee, surveying with eager interest the various specimens of horses, cattle, pigs, and model farms portrayed in the volume before me. I glanced at his mother now and then, to see how she relished the new-sprung intimacy; and I saw, by the unquiet aspect of her eye, that for some reason or other she was uneasy at the child's position.

"Arthur," said she, at length, "come here. You are troublesome to Mr. Markham: he wishes to read."

"By no means, Mrs. Graham; pray let him stay. I am as much amused as he is," pleaded I. But still, with hand and eye, she silently called him to her side.

"No, mamma," said the child; "let me look at these pictures first; and then I'll come and tell you all about them."

"We are going to have a small party on Monday, the fifth of November," said my mother; "and I hope you will not refuse to make one, Mrs. Graham. You can bring your little boy with you, you know—I daresay we shall be able to amuse him; and then you can make your own apologies to the Millwards and Wilsons—they will all be here, I expect."

"Thank you, I never go to parties."

"Oh! but this will be quite a family concern—early hours, and nobody here but ourselves, and just the Millwards and Wilsons, most of whom you already know, and Mr. Lawrence, your landlord, with whom you ought to make acquaintance."

"I do know something of him—but you must excuse me this time; for the evenings, now, are dark and damp, and Arthur, I fear, is too delicate to risk exposure to their influence with impunity. We must defer the enjoyment of your hospitality, till the return of longer days and warmer nights."

Rose, now, at a hint from my mother, produced a decanter of wine, with accompaniments of glasses and cake, from the cupboard and the oak sideboard, and the refreshment was duly presented to the guests. They both partook of the cake, but obstinately refused the wine, in spite of their hostess's hospitable attempts to force it upon them. Arthur, especially, shrank from the ruby nectar as if in terror and disgust, and was ready to cry when urged to take it.

"Never mind, Arthur," said his mamma, "Mrs. Markham thinks it will do you good, as you were tired with your walk, but she will not oblige you to take! I daresay you will do very well without. He detests the very sight of wine," she added, "and the smell of it almost makes him sick. I have been accustomed to make him swallow a little wine or weak spirits-and-water, by way of medicine when he was sick, and, in fact, I have done what I could to make him hate them."

Everybody laughed, except the young widow and her son.

"Well, Mrs. Graham," said my mother, wiping the tears of merriment from her bright blue eyes, "well, you surprise me! I really gave you credit for having more sense. The poor child will be the veriest milksop that ever was sopped! Only think what a man you will make of him, if you persist in—"

"I think it a very excellent plan," interrupted Mrs. Graham with imperturbable gravity. "By that means I hope to save him from one degrading vice at least. I wish I could render the incentives to every other equally innoxious in his case."

"But by such means," said I, "you will never render him virtuous. What is it that constitutes virtue, Mrs. Graham? Is it the circumstance of being able and willing to resist temptation; or that of having no temptations to resist? Is he a strong man that overcomes great obstacles and performs surprising achievements, though by dint of great muscular exertion, and at the risk of some subsequent fatigue, or he that sits in his chair all day, with nothing to do more laborious than stirring the fire, and carrying his food to his mouth? If you would have your son to walk honourably through the world, you must not attempt to clear the stones from his path, but teach him to walk firmly over them—not insist upon leading him by the hand, but let him learn to go alone."

"I will lead him by the hand, Mr. Markham, till he has strength to go alone; and I will clear as many stones from his path as I can, and teach him to avoid the rest—or walk firmly over them, as you say;—for when I have done my utmost, in the way of clearance, there will still be plenty left to exercise all the agility, steadiness, and circumspection he will ever have. It is all very well to talk about noble resistance, and trials of virtue, but for fifty—or five hundred men that have yielded to temptation, show me one that has had virtue to resist. And why should I take it for granted that my son will be one in a thousand? and not rather prepare for the worst, and suppose he will be like his—like the rest of mankind, unless I take care to prevent it?"

"You are very complimentary to us all," I observed.

"I know nothing about you—I speak of those I do know—and when I see the whole race of mankind (with a few rare exceptions) stumbling and blundering along the path of life, sinking into every pitfall, and breaking their shins over every impediment that lies in their way, shall I not use all the means in my power to ensure for him a smoother and safer passage?"

"Yes, but the surest means will be to endeavour to fortify him against temptation, not to remove it out of his way."

"I will do both, Mr. Markham. God knows he will have temptations enough to assail him, both from within and without, when I have done all I can to render vice as uninviting to him, as it is abominable in its own nature. I myself have had, indeed, but few incentives to what the world calls vice, but yet I have experienced temptations and trials of another kind, that have required, on many occasions, more watchfulness and firmness to resist than I have hitherto been able to muster against them. And this, I believe, is what most others would acknowledge, who are accustomed to reflection, and wishful to strive against their natural corruptions."

"Yes," said my mother, but half apprehending her drift; "but you would not judge of a boy by yourself—and, my dear Mrs. Graham, let me warn you in good time against the error—the fatal error, I may call it—of taking that boy's education upon yourself. Because you are clever in some things, and well-informed, you may fancy yourself equal to the task; but indeed you are not, and if you persist in the attempt, believe me you will bitterly repent it when the mischief is done."

"I am to send him to school, I suppose, to learn to despise his mother's authority and affection!" said the lady, with rather a bitter smile.

"Oh, no! But if you would have a boy to despise his mother, let her keep him at home, and spend her life in petting him up, and slaving to indulge his follies and caprices."

"I perfectly agree with you, Mrs. Markham; but nothing can be further from my principles and practice than such criminal weakness as that."

"Well, but you will treat him like a girl; you'll spoil his spirit, and make a mere Miss Nancy of him; you will indeed, Mrs. Graham, whatever you may think. But I'll get Mr. Millward to talk to you about it: he'll tell you the consequences; he'll set it before you as plain as the day, and tell you what you ought to do, and all about it; and, I don't doubt, he'll be able to convince you in a minute."

"No occasion to trouble the vicar," said Mrs. Graham, glancing at me—I suppose I was smiling at my mother's unbounded confidence in that worthy gentleman—"Mr. Markham here thinks his powers of conviction at least equal to Mr. Millward's. If I hear not him, neither should I be convinced though one rose from the dead, he would tell you. Well, Mr. Markham, you that maintain that a boy should not be shielded from evil, but sent out to battle against it, alone and unassisted; not taught to avoid the snares of life, but boldly to rush into them, or over them, as he may; to seek danger rather than shun it, and feed his virtue by temptation—would you——"

"I beg your pardon, Mrs. Graham, but you get on too fast. I have not yet said that a boy should be taught to rush into the snares of life—or even wilfully to seek temptation for the sake of exercising his virtue by overcoming it; I only say that it is better to arm and strengthen your hero, than to disarm and enfeeble the foe; and if you were to rear an oak sapling in a hothouse, tending it carefully night and day, and shielding it from every breath of wind, you could not expect it to become a hardy tree, like that which has grown up on the mountain-side, exposed to all the action of the elements, and not even sheltered from the shock of the tempest."

"Granted; but would you use the same argument with regard to a girl?"

"Certainly not."

"No: you would have her to be tenderly and delicately nurtured like a hothouse plant; taught to cling to others for direction and support, and guarded, as much as possible, from the very knowledge of evil. But will you be so good as to inform me why you make this distinction? Is it that you think she has no virtue?"

"Assuredly not."

"Well, but you affirm that virtue is only elicited by temptation; and you think that a woman cannot be too little exposed to temptation, or too little acquainted with vice, or anything connected therewith. It must be, either that you think she is essentially so vicious, or so feeble-minded that she cannot withstand temptation—and though she may be pure and innocent as long as she is kept in ignorance and restraint, yet, being destitute of real virtue, to teach her how to sin is at once to make her a sinner, and the greater her knowledge, the wider her liberty, the deeper will be her depravity; whereas, in the nobler sex, there is a natural tendency to goodness, guarded by a superior fortitude, which, the more it is exercised by trials and dangers, is only the further developed——"

"Heaven forbid that I should think so!" I interrupted her at last.

"Well then, it must be that you think they are both weak and prone to err, and the slightest error, the merest shadow of pollution, will ruin the one, while the character of the other will be strengthened and embellished—his education properly finished by a little practical acquaintance with forbidden things. Such experience, to him (to use a trite simile) will be like the storm to the oak, which, though it may scatter the leaves, and snap the smaller branches, serves but to rivet the roots, and to harden and condense the fibres of the tree. You would have us encourage our sons to prove all things by their own experience, while our daughters must not even profit by the experience of others. Now I would have both so to benefit by the experience of others, and the precepts of a higher authority, that they should know beforehand to refuse the evil and choose the good, and require no experimental proofs to teach them the evil of transgression. I would not send a poor girl into the world unarmed against her foes, and ignorant of the snares that beset her path; nor would I watch and guard her till, deprived of self-respect and self-reliance, she lost the power or the will to watch and guard herself; and as for my son—if I thought he would grow up to be what you call a man of the world—one that has 'seen life,' and glories in his experience, even though he should so far profit by it as to sober down, at length, into a useful and respected member of society—I would rather that he died tomorrow!—rather a thousand times!" she earnestly repeated, pressing her darling to her side and kissing his forehead with intense affection. He had, already, left his new companion, and been standing for some time beside his mother's knee, looking up into her face, and listening in silent wonder to her incomprehensible discourse.

"Well! you ladies must always have the last word, I suppose," said I, observing her rise, and begin to take leave of my mother.

"You may have as many words as you please—only I can't stay to hear them."

"No: that is the way: you hear just as much of an argument as you please; and the rest may be spoken to the wind."

"If you are anxious to say anything more on the subject," replied she, as she shook hands with Rose, "you must bring your sister to see me some fine day, and I'll listen, as patiently as you could wish, to whatever you please to say. I would rather be lectured by you than the vicar, because I should have less remorse in telling you, at the end of the discourse, that I preserve my own opinion precisely the same as at the beginning—as would be the case, I am persuaded, with regard to either logician."

"Yes, of course," replied I, determined to be as provoking as herself; "for, when a lady does consent to listen to an argument against her own opinions, she is always predetermined to withstand it—to listen only with her bodily ears, keeping the mental organs resolutely closed against the strongest reasoning."

"Good-morning, Mr. Markham," said my fair antagonist, with a pitying smile; and deigning no further rejoinder, she slightly bowed, and was about to withdraw; but her son, with childish impertinence, arrested her by exclaiming:

"Mamma, you have not shaken hands with Mr. Markham!"

She laughingly turned round, and held out her hand. I gave it a spiteful squeeze; for I was annoyed at the continual injustice she had done me from the very dawn of our acquaintance. Without knowing anything about my real disposition and principles, she was evidently prejudiced against me, and seemed bent upon showing me that her opinions respecting me, on every particular, fell far below those I entertained of myself. I was naturally touchy, or it would not have vexed me so much. Perhaps, too, I was a little bit spoiled by my mother and sister, and some other ladies of my acquaintance;—and yet I was by no means a fop—of that I am fully convinced, whether you are or not.

"Marmee's Lessons"

from *Little Women*

Louisa May Alcott

When they had laughed at Beth's story, they asked their mother for one; and, after a moment's thought, she said soberly,—

"As I sat cutting out blue flannel jackets to-day, at the rooms, I felt very anxious about father, and thought how lonely and helpless we should be if anything happened to him. It was not a wise thing to do, but I kept on worrying, till an old man came in with an order for some things. He sat down near me, and I began to talk to him, for he looked poor, and tired, and anxious.

" 'Have you sons in the army?' I asked, for the note he brought was not to me.

" 'Yes, ma'am; I had four, but two were killed; one is a prisoner, and I'm going to the other, who is very sick in a Washington hospital,' he answered, quietly.

" 'You have done a great deal for your country, sir,' I said, feeling respect now, instead of pity.

" 'Not a mite more than I ought ma'am. I'd go myself, if I was any use; as I ain't, I give my boys, and give 'em free.'

"He spoke so cheerfully, looked so sincere, and seemed so glad to give his all, that I was ashamed of myself. I'd given one man, and thought it too much, while he gave four, without grudging them; I had all my girls to comfort me at home, and his last son was waiting, miles away, to say 'good-by' to him, perhaps. I felt so rich, so happy, thinking of my blessings, that I made him a nice bundle, gave him some money, and thanked him heartily for the lesson he had taught me."

"Tell another story, mother; one with a moral to it, like this. I like to think about them afterwards, if they are real, and not too preachy," said Jo, after a minute's silence.

Mrs. March smiled, and began at once; for she had told stories to this little audience for many years, and knew how to please them.

"Once upon a time there were four girls, who had enough to eat, and drink, and wear; a good many comforts and pleasures, kind friends and parents, who loved them dearly, and yet they were not contented." (Here the listeners stole sly looks at one another, and began to sew diligently.) "These girls were anxious to be good, and made many excellent resolutions, but somehow they did not keep them very well, and were constantly saying, 'If we only had this,' or 'if we could only do that,' quite forgetting how much they already had, and how many pleasant things they actually could do; so they asked an old woman what spell they could use to make them happy, and she said, 'When you feel discontented, think over your blessings, and be grateful.' " (Here Jo looked up quickly, as if about to speak, but changed her mind, seeing that the story was not done yet.)

"Being sensible girls, they decided to try her advice, and soon were surprised to see how well off they were. One discovered that money couldn't keep shame and sorrow out of rich people's houses; another that though she was poor, she was a great deal happier with her youth, health, and good spirits, than a certain fretful, feeble old lady, who couldn't enjoy her comforts; a third, that, disagreeable as it was to help get dinner, it was harder still to have to go begging for it; and the fourth, that even carnelian rings were not so valuable as good behavior. So they agreed to stop complaining, to enjoy the blessings already possessed, and try to deserve them, lest they should be taken away entirely, instead of increased; and I believe they were never disappointed, or sorry that they took the old woman's advice."

"Now, Marmee, that is very cunning of you to turn our own stories against us, and give us a sermon instead of a 'spin,' " cried Meg.

"I like that kind of sermon; it's the sort father used to tell us," said Beth, thoughtfully, putting the needles straight on Jo's cushion.

"I don't complain near as much as the others do, and I shall be more careful than ever now, for I've had warning from Susie's downfall," said Amy, morally.

"We needed that lesson, and we won't forget it. If we do, you just say to us as Old Chloe did in Uncle Tom,—'Tink ob yer marcies, chillen, tink ob yer marcies,' " added Jo, who could not for the life of her help getting a morsel of fun out of the little sermon, though she took it to heart as much as any of them.

* * *

"Are you sure she is safe?" whispered Jo, looking remorsefully at the golden head, which might have been swept away from her sight forever, under the treacherous ice.

"Quite safe, dear; she is not hurt, and won't even take cold, I think, you were so sensible in covering and getting her home quickly," replied her mother, cheerfully.

"Laurie did it all; I only let her go. Mother, if she *should* die, it would be my fault;" and Jo dropped down beside the bed, in a passion of penitent tears, telling all that had happened, bitterly condemning her hardness of heart, and sobbing out her gratitude for being spared the heavy punishment which might have come upon her.

"It's my dreadful temper! I try to cure it; I think I have, and then it breaks out worse than ever. Oh, mother! what shall I do! what shall I do?" cried poor Jo, in despair.

"Watch and pray, dear; never get tired of trying; and never think it is impossible to conquer your fault," said Mrs. March, drawing the blowzy head to her shoulder, and kissing the wet cheek so tenderly, that Jo cried harder than ever.

"You don't know; you can't guess how bad it is! It seems as if I could do anything when I'm in a passion; I get so savage, I could hurt any one, and enjoy it. I'm afraid I *shall* do something dreadful some day, and spoil my life, and make everybody hate me. Oh, mother! help me, do help me!"

"I will, my child; I will. Don't cry so bitterly, but remember this day, and resolve, with all your soul, that you will never know another like it. Jo, dear, we all have our temptations, some far greater than yours, and it often takes us all our lives to conquer them. You think your temper is the worst in the world; but mine used to be just like it."

"Yours, mother? Why, you are never angry!" and, for the moment, Jo forgot remorse in surprise.

"I've been trying to cure it for forty years, and have only succeeded in controlling it. I am angry nearly every day of my life, Jo; but I have learned not to show it; and I still hope to learn not to feel it, though it may take me another forty years to do so."

The patience and the humility of the face she loved so well, was a better lesson to Jo than the wisest lecture, the sharpest reproof. She felt comforted at once by the sympathy and confidence given her; the knowledge that her mother had a fault like hers, and tried to mend it, made her own easier to bear, and strengthened her resolution to cure it; though forty years seemed rather a long time to watch and pray, to a girl of fifteen.

"Mother, are you angry when you fold your lips tight together, and go out of the room sometimes, when Aunt March scolds, or people worry you?" asked Jo, feeling nearer and dearer to her mother than ever before.

"Yes, I've learned to check the hasty words that rise to my lips; and when I feel that they mean to break out against my will, I just go away a minute, and give myself a little shake, for being so weak and wicked," answered Mrs. March, with a sigh and a smile, as she smoothed and fastened up Jo's dishevelled hair.

"How did you learn to keep still? That is what troubles me—for the sharp words fly out before I know what I'm about; and the more I say the worse I get, till it's a pleasure to hurt people's feelings, and say dreadful things. Tell me how you do it, Marmee dear."

"My good mother used to help me—"

"As you do us—" interrupted Jo, with a grateful kiss.

"But I lost her when I was a little older than you are, and for years had to struggle on alone, for I was too proud to confess my weakness to any one else. I had a hard time, Jo, and shed a good many bitter tears over my failures; for, in spite of my efforts, I never seemed to get on. Then your father came, and I was so happy that I found it easy to be good. But by and by, when I had four little daughters round me, and we were poor, then the old trouble began again; for I am not patient by nature, and it tried me very much to see my children wanting anything."

"Poor mother! what helped you then?"

"Your father, Jo. He never loses patience,—never doubts or complains,—but always hopes, and works and waits so cheerfully, that one is ashamed to do otherwise before him. He helped and comforted me, and showed me that I must try to practise all the virtues I would have my little girls possess, for I was their example. It was easier to try for your sakes than for my own; a startled or surprised look from one of you, when I spoke sharply, rebuked me more than any words could have done; and the love, respect, and confidence of my children was the sweetest reward I could receive for my efforts to be the woman I would have them copy."

"Oh, mother! if I'm ever half as good as you, I shall be satisfied," cried Jo, much touched.

"I hope you will be a great deal better, dear; but you must keep watch over your 'bosom enemy,' as father calls it, or it may sadden, if not spoil your life. You have had a warning; remember it, and try with heart and soul to master this quick temper, before it brings you greater sorrow and regret than you have known today."

"I will try, mother; I truly will. But you must help me, remind me, and keep me from flying out. I used to see father sometimes put his finger on his lips, and look at you with a very kind, but sober face; and you always folded your lips tight, or went away; was he reminding you then?" asked Jo, softly.

"Yes; I asked him to help me so, and he never forgot it, but saved me from many a sharp word by that little gesture and kind look."

Jo saw that her mother's eyes filled, and her lips trembled, as she spoke; and, fearing that she had said too much, she whispered anxiously, "Was it wrong to watch you, and to speak of it? I didn't mean to be rude, but it's so comfortable to say all I think to you, and feel so safe and happy here."

"My Jo, you may say anything to your mother, for it is my greatest happiness and pride to feel that my girls confide in me, and know how much I love them."

"I thought I'd grieved you."

"No, dear; but speaking of father reminded me how much I miss him, how much I owe him, and how faithfully I should watch and work to keep his little daughters safe and good for him."

"Yet you told him to go, mother, and didn't cry when he went, and never complain now, or seem as if you needed any help," said Jo, wondering.

"I gave my best to the country I love, and kept my tears till he was gone. Why should I complain, when we both have merely done our duty, and will surely be the happier for it in the end? If I don't seem to need help, it is because I have a better friend, even than father, to comfort and sustain me. My child, the troubles and temptations of your life are beginning, and may be many; but you can overcome and outlive them all, if you learn to feel the strength and tenderness of your Heavenly Father as you do that of your earthly one. The more you love and trust Him, the nearer you will feel to Him, and the less you will depend on human power and wisdom. His love and care never tire or change, can never be taken from you, but may become the source of lifelong peace, happiness, and strength. Believe this heartily, and go to God with all your little cares, and hopes, and sins, and sorrows, as freely and confidingly as you come to your mother."

Jo's only answer was to hold her mother close, and, in the silence which followed, the sincerest prayer she had ever prayed left her heart, without words; for in that sad, yet happy hour, she had learned not only the bitterness of remorse and despair, but the sweetness of self-denial and self-control; and, led by her mother's hand, she had drawn nearer to the Friend who welcomes every child with a love stronger than that of any father, tenderer than that of any mother.

Amy stirred, and sighed in her sleep; and, as if eager to begin at once to mend her fault, Jo looked up with an expression on her face which it had never worn before.

"I let the sun go down on my anger; I wouldn't forgive her, and today, if it hadn't been for Laurie, it might have been too late! How could I be so wicked?" said Jo, half aloud, as she leaned over her sister, softly stroking the wet hair scattered on the pillow.

As if she heard, Amy opened her eyes, and held out her arms, with a smile that went straight to Jo's heart. Neither said a word, but they hugged one another close, in spite of the blankets, and everything was forgiven and forgotten in one hearty kiss.

* * *

"What a dreadful day this has been!" begun Jo, usually the first to speak.

"It has seemed shorter than usual, but *so* uncomfortable," said Meg.

"Not a bit like home," added Amy.

"It can't seem so without Marmee and little Pip," sighed Beth, glancing, with full eyes, at the empty cage above her head.

"Here's mother, dear, and you shall have another bird to-morrow, if you want it."

As she spoke, Mrs. March came and took her place among them, looking as if her holiday had not been much pleasanter than theirs.

"Are you satisfied with your experiment, girls, or do you want another week of it?" she asked, as Beth nestled up to her, and the rest turned toward her with brightening faces, as flowers turn toward the sun.

"I don't!" cried Jo, decidedly.

"Nor I," echoed the others.

"You think, then, that it is better to have a few duties, and live a little for others, do you?"

"Lounging and larking don't pay," observed Jo, shaking her head. "I'm tired of it, and mean to go to work at something right off."

"Suppose you learn plain cooking; that's a useful accomplishment, which no woman should be without," said Mrs. March, laughing audibly at the recollection of Jo's dinner-party; for she had met Miss Crocker, and heard her account of it.

"Mother! did you go away and let everything be, just to see how we'd get on?" cried Meg, who had had suspicions all day.

"Yes; I wanted you to see how the comfort of all depends on each doing their share faithfully. While Hannah and I did your work, you got on pretty well, though I don't think you were very happy or amiable; so I thought, as a little lesson, I would show you what happens when every one thinks only of herself. Don't you feel that it is pleasanter to help one another, to have daily duties which make leisure sweet when it comes, and to bear or forbear, that home may be comfortable and lovely to us all?"

"We do, mother, we do!" cried the girls.

"Then let me advise you to take up your little burdens again; for though they seem heavy sometimes, they are good for us, and lighten as we learn to carry them. Work is wholesome, and there is plenty for every one; it keeps us from *ennui* and mischief; is good for health and spirits, and gives us a sense of power and independence better than money or fashion."

"We'll work like bees, and love it too; see if we don't!" said Jo. "I'll learn plain cooking for my holiday task; and the next dinner-party I have shall be a success."

"I'll make the set of shirts for father, instead of letting you do it, Marmee. I can and I will, though I'm not fond of sewing; that will be better than fussing over my own things, which are plenty nice enough as they are," said Meg.

"I'll do my lessons every day, and not spend so much time with my music and dolls. I am a stupid thing, and ought to be studying, not playing," was Beth's resolution; while Amy followed their example, by heroically declaring, "I shall learn to make buttonholes, and attend to my parts of speech."

"Very good! then I am quite satisfied with the experiment, and fancy that we shall not have to repeat it; only don't go to the other extreme, and delve like slaves. Have regular hours for work and play; make each day both useful and pleasant, and prove that you understand the worth of time by employing it well. Then youth will be delightful, old age will bring few regrets, and life become a beautiful success, in spite of poverty."

"We'll remember, mother!" and they did.

* * *

"Now, grandma's sixtieth birthday! Long life to her, with three times three!"

That was given with a will, as you may well believe; and the cheering once begun, it was hard to stop it. Everybody's health was proposed, from Mr. Laurence, who was considered their special patron, to the astonished guinea-pig, who had strayed from its proper sphere in search of its young master. Demi, as the oldest grandchild, then presented the queen of the day with various gifts, so numerous that they were transported to the festive scene in a wheelbarrow. Funny presents, some of them, but what would have been defects to other eyes were ornaments to grandma's,—for the children's gifts were all their own. Every stitch Daisy's patient little fingers had put into the handkerchiefs she hemmed, was better than embroidery to Mrs. March; Demi's shoe-box was a miracle of mechanical skill, though the cover wouldn't shut; Rob's footstool had a wiggle in its uneven legs, that she declared was very soothing; and no page of the costly book Amy's child gave her, was so fair as that on which appeared, in tipsy capitals, the words,—"To dear Grandma, from her little Beth."

During this ceremony the boys had mysteriously disappeared; and, when Mrs. March had tried to thank her children, and broken down, while Teddy wiped her eyes on his pinafore, the Professor suddenly began to sing. Then, from above him, voice after voice took up the words, and from tree to tree echoed the music of the unseen choir, as the boys sung, with all their hearts, the little song Jo had written, Laurie set to music, and the Professor trained his lads to give with the best effect. This was something altogether new, and it proved a grand success, for Mrs. March couldn't get over her surprise, and insisted on shaking hands with every one of the featherless birds, from tall Franz and Emil to the little quadroon, who had the sweetest voice of all.

After this, the boys dispersed for a final lark, leaving Mrs. March and her daughters under the festival tree.

"I don't think I ever ought to call myself 'Unlucky Jo' again, when my greatest wish has been so beautifully gratified," said Mrs. Bhaer, taking Teddy's little fist out of the milk pitcher, in which he was rapturously churning.

"And yet your life is very different from the one you pictured so long ago. Do you remember our castles in the air?" asked Amy, smiling as she watched Laurie and John playing cricket with the boys.

"Dear fellows! It does my heart good to see them forget business, and frolic for a day," answered Jo, who now spoke in a maternal way of all mankind. "Yes, I remember; but the life I wanted then seems selfish, lonely and cold to me now. I haven't given up the hope that I may write a good book yet, but I can wait, and I'm sure it will be all the better for such experiences and illustrations as these;" and Jo pointed from the lively lads in the distance to her father, leaning on the Professor's arm, as they walked to and fro in the sunshine, deep in one of the conversations which both enjoyed so much, and then to her mother, sitting enthroned among her daughters, with their children in her lap and at her feet, as if all found help and happiness in the face which never could grow old to them.

"My castle was the most nearly realized of all. I asked for splendid things, to be sure, but in my heart I knew I should be satisfied, if I had a little home, and John, and some dear children like these. I've got them all, thank God, and am the happiest woman in the world;" and Meg laid her hand on her tall boy's head, with a face full of tender and devout content.

"My castle is very different from what I planned, but I would not alter it, though, like Jo, I don't relinquish all my artistic hopes, or confine myself to helping others fulfil their dreams of beauty. I've begun to model a figure of baby, and Laurie says it is the best thing I've ever done. I think so myself, and mean to do it in marble, so that whatever happens, I may at least keep the image of my little angel."

As Amy spoke, a great tear dropped on the golden hair of the sleeping child in her arms; for her one well-beloved daughter was a frail little creature, and the dread of losing her was the shadow over Amy's sunshine. This cross was doing much for both father and mother, for one love and sorrow bound them closely together. Amy's nature was growing sweeter, deeper and more tender; Laurie was growing more serious, strong and firm, and both were learning that beauty, youth, good fortune, even love itself, cannot keep care and pain, loss and sorrow, from the most blest; for—

"Into each life some rain must fall,
Some days must be dark, and sad, and dreary."

"She is growing better, I am sure of it, my dear; don't despond, but hope, and keep happy," said Mrs. March, as tender-hearted Daisy stooped from her knee, to lay her rosy cheek against her little cousin's pale one.

"I never ought to, while I have you to cheer me up, Marmee, and Laurie to take more than half of every burden," replied Amy, warmly. "He never lets me see his anxiety, but is so sweet and patient with me, so devoted to Beth, and such a stay and comfort to me always, that I can't love him enough. So, in spite of my one cross, I can say with Meg, 'Thank God, I'm a happy woman.' "

"There's no need for me to say it, for every one can see that I'm far happier than I deserve," added Jo, glancing from her good husband to her chubby children, tumbling on the grass beside her. "Fritz is getting gray and stout, I'm growing as thin as a shadow, and am over thirty; we never shall be rich, and Plumfield may burn up any night, for that incorrigible Tommy Bangs *will* smoke sweet-fern cigars under the bedclothes, though he's set himself afire three times already. But in spite of these unromantic facts, I have nothing to complain of, and never was so jolly in my life. Excuse the remark, but living among boys, I can't help using their expressions now and then."

"Yes, Jo, I think your harvest will be a good one," began Mrs. March, frightening away a big black cricket, that was staring Teddy out of countenance.

"Not half so good as yours, mother. Here it is, and we never can thank you enough for the patient sowing and reaping you have done," cried Jo, with the loving impetuosity which she never could outgrow.

"I hope there will be more wheat and fewer tares every year," said Amy, softly.

"A large sheaf, but I know there's room in your heart for it, Marmee dear," added Meg's tender voice.

Touched to the heart, Mrs. March could only stretch out her arms, as if to gather children and grandchildren to herself, and say, with face and voice full of motherly love, gratitude, and humility,—

"Oh, my girls, however long you may live, I never can wish you a greater happiness than this!"

"Huckleberries"

from *Little Men*

Louisa May Alcott

There was a great clashing of tin pails, much running to and fro, and frequent demands for something to eat, one August afternoon, for the boys were going huckleberrying, and made as much stir about it as if they were setting out to find the Northwest Passage.

"Now, my lads, get off as quietly as you can, for Rob is safely out of the way, and won't see you," said Mrs. Bhaer, as she tied Daisy's broad-brimmed hat, and settled the great blue pinafore in which she had enveloped Nan.

But the plan did not succeed, for Rob had heard the bustle, decided to go, and prepared himself, without a thought of disappointment. The troop was just getting under way when the little man came marching downstairs with his best hat on, a bright tin pail in his hand, and a face beaming with satisfaction.

"Oh, dear! now we shall have a scene," sighed Mrs. Bhaer, who found her eldest son very hard to manage at times.

"I'm all ready," said Rob, and took his place in the ranks with such perfect unconsciousness of his mistake, that it really was very hard to undeceive him.

"It's too far for you, my love; stay and take care of me, for I shall be all alone," began his mother.

"You have Teddy. I'm a big boy, so I can go; you said I might when I was bigger, and I am now," persisted Rob, with a cloud beginning to dim the brightness of his happy face.

"We are going up to the great pasture, and it's ever so far; we don't want you tagging on," cried Jack, who did not admire the little boys.

"I won't tag, I'll run and keep up. Oh, mamma! let me go! I want to fill my new pail, and I'll bring them all to you. Please, please, I will be good!" prayed Robby, looking up at his mother, so grieved and disappointed that her heart began to fail her.

"But, my dear, you'll get so tired and hot you won't have a good time. Wait till I go, and then we will stay all day, and pick as many berries as you want."

"You never do go, you are so busy and I'm tired of waiting. I'd rather go and get the berries for you all myself. I love to pick them, and I want to fill my new pail dreffly," sobbed Rob.

The pathetic sight of great tears tinkling into the dear new pail, and threatening to fill it with salt water instead of huckleberries, touched all the ladies present. His mother patted the weeper on his back; Daisy offered to stay at home with him; and Nan said, in her decided way:

"Let him come; I'll take care of him."

"If Franz were going I wouldn't mind, for he is very careful; but he is haying with the father, and I'm not sure about the rest of you," began Mrs. Bhaer.

"It's so far," put in Jack.

"I'd carry him if I were going—wish I were," said Dan, with a sigh.

"Thank you, dear, but you must take care of your foot. I wish I could go. Stop a minute, I think I can manage it after all," and Mrs. Bhaer ran out to the steps, waving her apron wildly.

Silas was just driving away in the hay cart, but turned back, and agreed at once, when Mrs. Jo proposed that he should take the whole party to the pasture, and go for them at five o'clock.

"It will delay your work a little, but never mind; we will pay you in huckleberry pies," said Mrs. Jo, knowing Silas's weak point.

His rough, brown face brightened up, and he said, with a cheery, "Haw! haw! Wal now, Mis Bhaer, if you go to bribin' of me, I shall give in right away."

"Now, boys, I have arranged it so that you can all go," said Mrs. Bhaer, running back again, much relieved, for she loved to make them happy, and always felt miserable when she had disturbed the serenity of her little sons; for she believed that the small hopes and plans and pleasures of children should be tenderly respected by grown-up people, and never rudely thwarted or ridiculed.

"May I go?" said Dan, delighted.

"I thought especially of you. Be careful, and never mind the berries, but sit about and enjoy the lovely things which you know how to find all about you," answered Mrs. Bhaer, who remembered his kind offer to her boy.

"Me too! me too!" sung Rob, dancing with joy, and clapping his precious pail and cover like castanets.

"Yes, and Daisy and Nan must take good care of you. Be at the bars at five o'clock, and Silas will come for you all."

Robby cast himself upon his mother in a burst of gratitude, promising to bring her every berry he picked, and not eat one. Then they were all packed into the hay cart, and went rattling away, the brightest face among the dozen being that of Rob, as he sat between his two temporary little mothers, beaming upon the whole world, and waving his best hat; for his indulgent mamma had not the heart to bereave him of it, since this was a gala day to him.

Such a happy afternoon as they had, in spite of the mishaps which usually occur on such expeditions! Of course Tommy came to grief, tumbled upon a hornets' nest and got stung; but being used to woe, he bore the smart manfully, till Dan suggested the application of damp earth, which much assuaged the pain. Daisy saw a snake, and in flying from it lost half her berries; but Demi helped her to fill up again, and discussed reptiles most learnedly the while. Ned fell out of a tree, and split his jacket down the back, but suffered no other fracture. Emil and Jack established rival claims to a certain thick patch, and while they were squabbling about it, Stuffy quickly and quietly stripped the bushes and fled to the protection of Dan, who was enjoying himself immensely. The crutch was no longer necessary, and he was delighted to see how strong his foot felt as he roamed about the great pasture, full of interesting rocks and stumps, with familiar little creatures in the grass, and well-known insects dancing in the air.

But of all the adventures that happened on this afternoon that which befell Nan and Rob was the most exciting, and it long remained one of the favorite histories of the household. Having explored the country pretty generally, torn three rents in her frock, and scratched her face in a barberry bush, Nan began to pick the berries that shone like big, black beads on the low, green bushes. Her nimble fingers flew, but still her basket did not fill up as rapidly as she desired, so she kept wandering here and there to search for better places, instead of picking contentedly and steadily as Daisy did. Rob followed Nan, for her energy suited him better than his cousin's patience, and he too was anxious to have the biggest and best berries for mother.

"I keep putting them in, but it doesn't fill up, and I'm so tired," said Rob, pausing a moment to rest his short legs, and beginning to think huckleberrying was not all his fancy painted it; for the sun blazed, Nan skipped hither and thither like a grasshopper, and the berries fell out of his pail almost as fast as he put them in, because, in his struggles with the bushes, it was often upside down.

"Last time we came they were ever so much thicker over that wall—great bouncers; and there is a cave there, where the boys made a fire. Let's go and fill our things quick, and then hide in the cave and let the others find us," proposed Nan, thirsting for adventures.

Rob consented, and away they went, scrambling over the wall and running down the sloping fields on the other side, till they were hidden among the rocks and underbrush. The berries were thick, and at last the pails were actually full. It was shady and cool down there, and a little spring gave the thirsty children a refreshing drink out of its mossy cup.

"Now we will go and rest in the cave, and eat our lunch," said Nan, well satisfied with her success so far.

"Do you know the way?" asked Rob.

" 'Course I do; I've been once, and I always remember. Didn't I go and get my box all right?"

That convinced Rob, and he followed blindly as Nan led him over stock and stone, and brought him, after much meandering, to a small recess in the rock, where the blackened stones showed that fires had been made.

"Now, isn't it nice?" asked Nan, as she took out a bit of bread and butter, rather damaged by being mixed up with nails, fish hooks, stones, and other foreign substances, in the young lady's pocket.

"Yes; do you think they will find us soon?" asked Rob, who found the shadowy glen rather dull, and began to long for more society.

"No, I don't; because if I hear them, I shall hide, and have fun making them find me."

"P'raps they won't come."

"Don't care; I can get home myself."

"Is it a great way?" asked Rob, looking at his little, stubby boots, scratched and wet with his long wandering.

"It's six miles, I guess." Nan's ideas of distance were vague, and her faith in her own powers great.

"I think we better go now," suggested Rob, presently.

"I shan't go till I have picked over my berries," and Nan began what seemed to Rob an endless task.

"Oh, dear! you said you'd take good care of me," he sighed, as the sun seemed to drop behind the hill all of a sudden.

"Well, I *am* taking care of you as hard as I can. Don't be cross, child; I'll go in a minute," said Nan, who considered five-year-old Robby a mere infant compared to herself.

So little Rob sat looking anxiously about him, and waiting patiently, for, spite of some misgivings, he felt great confidence in Nan.

"I guess it's going to be night pretty soon," he observed, as if to himself, as a mosquito bit him, and the frogs in a neighboring marsh began to pipe up for the evening concert.

"My goodness me! so it is. Come right away this minute, or they will be gone," cried Nan, looking up from her work, and suddenly perceiving that the sun was down.

"I heard a horn about an hour ago; maybe they were blowing for us," said Rob, trudging after his guide as she scrambled up the steep hill.

"Where was it?" asked Nan, stopping short.

"Over that way," he pointed with a dirty little finger in an entirely wrong direction.

"Let's go that way and meet them," and Nan wheeled about, and began to trot through the bushes, feeling a trifle anxious, for there were so many cowpaths all about she could not remember which way they came.

On they went over stock and stone again, pausing now and then to listen for the horn, which did not blow any more, for it was only the moo of a cow on her way home.

"I don't remember seeing that pile of stones—do you?" asked Nan, as she sat on a wall to rest a moment and take an observation.

"I don't remember anything, but I want to go home," and Rob's voice had a little tremble in it that made Nan put her arms round him and lift him gently down, saying, in her most capable way:

"I'm going just as fast as I can, dear. Don't cry, and when we come to the road, I'll carry you."

"Where is the road?" and Robby wiped his eyes to look for it.

"Over by that big tree. Don't you know that's the one Ned tumbled out of?"

"So it is. Maybe they waited for us; I'd like to ride home—wouldn't you?" and Robby brightened up as he plodded along toward the end of the great pasture.

"No, I'd rather walk," answered Nan, feeling quite sure that she would be obliged to do so, and preparing her mind for it.

Another long trudge through the fast-deepening twilight and another disappointment, for when they reached the tree, they found to their dismay that it was not the one Ned climbed, and no road anywhere appeared.

"Are we lost?" quavered Rob, clasping his pail in despair.

"Not much. I don't just see which way to go, and I guess we'd better call."

So they both shouted till they were hoarse, yet nothing answered but the frogs in full chorus.

"There is another tall tree over there, perhaps that's the one," said Nan, whose heart sank within her, though she still spoke bravely.

"I don't think I can go any more; my boots are so heavy I can't pull them," and Robby sat down on a stone quite worn out.

"Then we must stay here all night. *I* don't care much, if snakes don't come."

"I'm frightened of snakes. I can't stay all night. Oh, dear! I don't like to be lost," and Rob puckered up his face to cry, when suddenly a thought occurred to him, and he said, in a tone of perfect confidence:

"Marmar will come and find me; she always does; I'm not afraid now."

"She won't know where we are."

"She didn't know I was shut up in the ice house, but she found me. I know she'll come," returned Robby, so trustfully, that Nan felt relieved, and sat down by him, saying, with a remorseful sigh:

"I wish we hadn't run away."

"You made me; but I don't mind much—Marmar will love me just the same," answered Rob, clinging to his sheet anchor when all other hope was gone.

"I'm so hungry. Let's eat our berries," proposed Nan after a pause, during which Rob began to nod.

"So am I, but I can't eat mine, 'cause I told Marmar I'd keep them all for her."

"You'll have to eat them if no one comes for us," said Nan, who felt like contradicting everything just then. "If we stay here a great many days, we shall eat up all the berries in the field, and then we shall starve," she added, grimly.

"I shall eat sassafras. I know a big tree of it, and Dan told me how squirrels dig up the roots and eat them, and I love to dig," returned Rob, undaunted by the prospect of starvation.

"Yes; and we can catch frogs, and cook them. My father ate some once, and he said they were nice," put in Nan, beginning to find a spice of romance even in being lost in a huckleberry pasture.

"How could we cook frogs? We haven't any fire."

"I don't know; next time I'll have matches in my pocket," said Nan, rather depressed by this obstacle to the experiment in frog cookery.

"Couldn't we light a fire with a firefly?" asked Rob, hopefully, as he watched them flitting to and fro like sparks.

"Let's try," and several minutes were pleasantly spent in catching the flies, and trying to make them kindle a green twig or two. "It's a lie to call them *fire*-flies when there isn't a fire in them," Nan said, throwing one unhappy insect away with scorn, though it shone its best, and obligingly walked up and down the twigs to please the innocent little experimenters.

"Marmar's a good while coming," said Rob, after another pause, during which they watched the stars overhead, smelled the sweet fern crushed underfoot, and listened to the cricket's serenade.

"I don't see why God made any night; day is so much pleasanter," said Nan, thoughtfully.

"It's to sleep in," answered Rob, with a yawn.

"Then do go to sleep," said Nan, pettishly.

"I want my own bed. Oh, I wish I could see Teddy!" cried Rob, painfully reminded of home by the soft chirp of birds safe in their little nests.

"I don't believe your mother will ever find us," said Nan, who was becoming desperate, for she hated patient waiting of any sort. "It's so dark she won't see us."

"It was all black in the ice house, and I was so scared I didn't call her, but she saw me; and she will see me now, no matter how dark it is," returned confiding Rob, standing up to peer into the gloom for the help which never failed him.

"I see her! I see her!" he cried, and ran as fast as his tired legs would take him toward a dark figure slowly approaching. Suddenly he stopped, then turned about, and came stumbling back, screaming, in a great panic:

"No, it's a bear, a big black one!" and hid his face in Nan's skirts.

For a moment Nan quailed; even her courage gave out at thought of a real bear, and she was about to turn and flee in great disorder, when a mild "Moo!" changed her fear to merriment, as she said, laughing:

"It's a cow, Robby! the nice, black cow we saw this afternoon."

The cow seemed to feel that it was not just the thing to meet two little people in her pasture after dark, and the amiable beast paused to inquire into the case. She let them stroke her, and stood regarding them with her soft eyes so mildly, that Nan, who feared no animal but a bear, was fired with a desire to milk her.

"Silas taught me how; and berries and milk would be so nice," she said, emptying the contents of her pail into her hat, and boldly beginning her new task, while Rob stood by and repeated, at her command, the poem from Mother Goose:

"Cushy cow, bonny, let down your milk,
Let down your milk to me,
And I will give you a gown of silk,
A gown of silk and a silver tee."

But the immortal rime had little effect, for the benevolent cow had already been milked, and had only half a gill to give the thirsty children.

"Shoo! get away! you are an old cross patch," cried Nan, ungratefully, as she gave up the attempt in despair; and poor Mooly walked on with a gentle gurgle of surprise and reproof.

"Each can have a sip, and then we must take a walk. We shall go to sleep if we don't; and lost people mustn't sleep. Don't you know how Hannah Lee in the pretty story slept under the snow and died?"

"But there isn't any snow now, and it's nice and warm," said Rob, who was not blessed with as lively a fancy as Nan.

"No matter, we will poke about a little, and call some more; and then, if nobody comes, we will hide under the bushes, like Hop-o'-my-thumb and his brothers."

It was a very short walk, however, for Rob was so sleepy he could not get on, and tumbled down so often that Nan entirely lost patience, being half distracted by the responsibility she had taken upon herself.

"If you tumble down again, I'll shake you," she said, lifting the poor little man up very kindly as she spoke, for Nan's bark was much worse than her bite.

"Please don't. It's my boots—they keep slipping so," and Rob manfully checked the sob just ready to break out, adding, with a plaintive patience that touched Nan's heart, "If the skeeters didn't bite me so, I could go to sleep till Marmar comes."

"Put your head on my lap, and I'll cover you up with my apron; I'm not afraid of the night," said Nan, sitting down and trying to persuade herself that she did not mind the shadow nor the mysterious rustlings all about her.

"Wake me up when she comes," said Rob, and was fast asleep in five minutes with his head in Nan's lap under the pinafore.

The little girl sat for some fifteen minutes, staring about her with anxious eyes, and feeling as if each second were an hour. Then a pale light began to glimmer over the hilltop, and she said to herself:

"I guess the night is over and morning is coming. I'd like to see the sun rise, so I'll watch, and when it comes up we can find our way right home."

But before the moon's round face peeped above the hill to destroy her hope, Nan had fallen asleep, leaning back in a little bower of tall ferns, and was deep in a midsummer night's dream of fireflies and blue aprons, mountains of huckleberries, and Robby wiping away the tears of a black cow, who sobbed, "I want to go home! I want to go home!"

While the children were sleeping, peacefully lulled by the drowsy hum of many neighborly mosquitoes, the family at home were in a great state of agitation. The hay cart came at five, and all but Jack, Emil, Nan, and Rob were at the bars ready for it. Franz drove instead of Silas, and when the boys told him that the others were going home through the wood, he said, looking ill-pleased, "They ought to have left Rob to ride, he will be tired out by the long walk."

"It's shorter that way, and they will carry him," said Stuffy, who was in a hurry for his supper.

"You are sure Nan and Rob went with them?"

"Of course they did; I saw them getting over the wall, and sung out that it was 'most five, and Jack called back that they were going the other way," explained Tommy.

"Very well, pile in then," and away rattled the hay cart with the tired children and the full pails.

Mrs. Jo looked sober when she heard of the division of the party, and sent Franz back with Toby to find and bring the little ones home. Supper was over, and the family sitting about in the cool hall as usual, when Franz came trotting back, hot, dusty, and anxious.

"Have they come?" he called out when halfway up the avenue.

"No!" and Mrs. Jo flew out of her chair looking so alarmed that everyone jumped up and gathered round Franz.

"I can't find them anywhere," he began; but the words were hardly spoken when a loud "Hullo!" startled them all, and the next minute Jack and Emil came round the house.

"Where are Nan and Rob?" cried Mrs. Jo, clutching Emil in a way that caused him to think his aunt had suddenly lost her wits.

"I don't know. They came home with the others, didn't they?" he answered, quickly.

"No; George and Tommy said they went with you."

"Well, they didn't. Haven't seen them. We took a swim in the pond, and came by the wood," said Jack, looking alarmed, as well he might.

"Call Mr. Bhaer, get the lanterns, and tell Silas I want him."

That was all Mrs. Jo said, but they knew what she meant, and flew to obey orders. In ten minutes, Mr. Bhaer and Silas were off to the wood, and Franz tearing down the road on Old Andy to search the great pasture. Mrs. Jo caught up some food from the table, a little bottle of brandy from the medicine closet, took a lantern, and bidding Jack and Emil come with her, and the rest not stir, she trotted away on Toby, never stopping for hat or shawl. She heard someone running after her, but said not a word till, as she paused to call and listen, the light of her lantern shone on Dan's face.

"You here! I told Jack to come," she said, half inclined to send him back, much as she needed help.

"I wouldn't let him; he and Emil hadn't had any supper, and I wanted to come more than they did," he said, taking the lantern from her and smiling up in her face with the steady look in his eyes that made her feel as if, boy though he was, she had someone to depend on.

Off she jumped, and ordered him on to Toby, in spite of his pleading to walk; then they went on again along the dusty, solitary road, stopping every now and then to call and hearken breathlessly for little voices to reply.

When they came to the great pasture, other lights were already flitting to and fro like will-o'-the-wisps, and Mr. Bhaer's voice was heard shouting, "Nan! Rob! Rob! Nan!" in every part of the field. Silas whistled and roared, Dan plunged here and there on Toby, who seemed to understand the case, and went over the roughest places with unusual docility. Often Mrs. Jo hushed them all, saying, with a sob in her throat, "The noise may frighten them, let me call; Robby will know *my* voice," and then she would cry out the beloved little name in every tone of tenderness, till the very echoes whispered it softly, and the winds seemed to waft it willingly; but still no answer came.

The sky was overcast now, and only brief glimpses of the moon were seen, heat lightning darted out of the dark clouds now and then, and a faint far-off rumble as of thunder told that a summer storm was brewing.

"Oh, my Robby! my Robby!" mourned poor Mrs. Jo, wandering up and down like a pale ghost, while Dan kept beside her like a faithful firefly. "What shall I say to Nan's father if she comes to harm? Why did I ever trust my darling so far away? Fritz, do you hear anything?" And when a mournful "No" came back, she wrung her hands so despairingly, that Dan sprung down from Toby's back, tied the bridle to the bars, and said, in his decided way:

"They may have gone down to the spring—I'm going to look."

He was over the wall and away so fast that she could hardly follow him; but when she reached the spot, he lowered the lantern and showed her with joy the marks of little feet in the soft ground about the spring. She fell down on her knees to examine the tracks, and then sprung up, saying eagerly:

"Yes; that is the mark of my Robby's little boots! Come this way, they must have gone on."

Such a weary search! But now some inexplicable instinct seemed to lead the anxious mother, for presently Dan uttered a cry, and caught up a little shining object lying in the path. It was the cover of the new tin pail, dropped in the first alarm of being lost. Mrs. Jo hugged and kissed it as if it were a living thing; and when Dan was about to utter a glad shout to bring the others to the spot, she stopped him, saying, as she hurried on, "No, let *me* find them; I let Rob go, and I want to give him back to his father all myself."

A little farther on Nan's hat appeared, and after passing the place more than once, they came at last upon the babes in the wood both sound asleep. Dan never forgot the little picture on which the light of his lantern shone that night. He thought Mrs. Jo would cry out, but she only whispered "Hush!" as she softly lifted away the apron, and saw the little ruddy face below. The berry-stained lips were half-open as the breath came and went, the yellow hair lay damp on the hot forehead, and both the chubby hands held fast the little pail, still full.

The sight of the childish harvest, treasured through all the troubles of that night for her, seemed to touch Mrs. Jo to the heart, for suddenly she gathered up her boy, and began to cry over him, so tenderly, yet so heartily, that he woke up, and at first seemed bewildered. Then he remembered, and hugged her close, saying with a laugh of triumph:

"I knew you'd come! Oh, Marmar! I did want you so!" For a moment they kissed and clung to one another, quite forgetting all the world; for no matter how lost and soiled and worn-out wandering sons may be, mothers can forgive and forget everything as they fold them in their fostering arms. Happy the son whose faith in his mother remains unchanged, and who, through all his wanderings, has kept some filial token to repay her brave and tender love.

Dan meantime picked Nan out of her bush, and, with a gentleness none but Teddy ever saw in him before, he soothed her first alarm at the sudden waking, and wiped away her tears; for Nan also began to cry for joy, it was so good to see a kind face and feel a strong arm round her after what seemed to her ages of loneliness and fear.

"My poor little girl, don't cry! You are all safe now, and no one shall say a word of blame tonight," said Mrs. Jo, taking Nan into her capacious embrace, and cuddling both children as a hen might gather her lost chickens under her motherly wings.

"It was my fault; but I *am* sorry. I tried to take care of him, and I covered him up and let him sleep, and didn't touch his berries, though I was so hungry; and I never will do it again—truly never, never," sobbed Nan, quite lost in a sea of penitence and thankfulness.

"Call them now, and let us get home," said Mrs. Jo; and Dan, getting upon the wall, sent the joyful word "Found!" ringing over the field.

How the wandering lights came dancing from all sides, and gathered round the little group among the sweet fern bushes! Such a hugging and kissing and talking and crying as went on must have amazed the glowworms, and evidently delighted the mosquitoes, for they hummed frantically, while the little moths came in flocks to the party, and the frogs croaked as if they could not express their satisfaction loudly enough.

Then they set out for home a queer party, for Franz rode on to tell the news; Dan and Toby led the way; then came Nan in the strong arms of Silas, who considered her "the smartest little baggage he ever saw," and teased her all the way home about her pranks. Mr. Bhaer would let no one carry Rob but himself, and the little fellow, refreshed by sleep, sat up, and chattered gayly, feeling himself a hero, while his mother went beside him, holding on to any part of his precious little body that came handy, and never tired of hearing him say, "I *knew* Marmar would come," or seeing him lean down to kiss her, and put a plump berry into her mouth, " 'Cause he picked them all for her."

The moon shone out just as they reached the avenue, and all the boys came shouting to meet them, so the lost lambs were borne in triumph and safety, and landed in the dining room, where the unromantic little things demanded supper instead of preferring kisses and caresses. They were set down to bread and milk, while the entire household stood round to gaze upon them. Nan soon recovered her spirits, and recounted her perils with a relish now that they were all over. Rob seemed absorbed in his food, but put down his spoon all of a sudden, and set up a doleful roar.

"My precious, why do you cry?" asked his mother, who still hung over him.

"I'm crying 'cause I was lost," bawled Rob, trying to squeeze out a tear, and failing entirely.

"But you are found now. Nan says you didn't cry out in the field, and I was glad you were such a brave boy."

"I was so busy being frightened I didn't have any time then. But I want to cry now, 'cause I don't like to be lost," explained Rob, struggling with sleep, emotion, and a mouthful of bread and milk.

The boys set up such a laugh at this funny way of making up for lost time, that Rob stopped to look at them, and the merriment was so infectious, that, after a surprised stare, he burst out into a merry "Ha, ha!" and beat his spoon upon the table as if he enjoyed the joke immensely.

"It is ten o'clock; into bed, every man of you," said Mr. Bhaer, looking at his watch.

"And, thank Heaven! there will be no empty ones tonight," added Mrs. Bhaer, watching, with full eyes, Robby going up in his father's arms, and Nan, escorted by Daisy and Demi, who considered her the most interesting heroine of their collection.

"Poor Aunt Jo is so tired she ought to be carried up herself," said gentle Franz, putting his arm round her as she paused at the stair foot, looking quite exhausted by her fright and long walk.

"Let's make an armchair," proposed Tommy.

"No, thank you, my lads; but somebody may lend me a shoulder to lean on," answered Mrs. Jo.

"Me! me!" and half a dozen jostled one another, all eager to be chosen, for there was something in the pale, motherly face that touched the warm hearts under the round jackets.

Seeing that they considered it an honor, Mrs. Jo gave it to the one who had earned it, and nobody grumbled when she put her arm on Dan's broad shoulder, saying, with a look that made him color up with pride and pleasure:

"He found the children; so I think he must help me up."

Dan felt richly rewarded for his evening's work, not only that he was chosen from all the rest to go proudly up bearing the lamp, but because

Mrs. Jo said, heartily, "Good night, my boy! God bless you!" as he left her at her door.

"I wish I *were* your boy," said Dan, who felt as if danger and trouble had somehow brought him nearer than ever to her.

"You shall be my oldest son," and she sealed her promise with a kiss that made Dan hers entirely.

Little Rob was all right next day, but Nan had a headache, and lay on Mother Bhaer's sofa with cold cream upon her scratched face. Her remorse was quite gone, and she evidently thought being lost rather a fine amusement. Mrs. Jo was not pleased with this state of things, and had no desire to have her children led from the paths of virtue, or her pupils lying round loose in huckleberry fields. So she talked soberly to Nan, and tried to impress upon her mind the difference between liberty and license, telling several tales to enforce her lecture. She had not decided how to punish Nan, but one of these stories suggested a way, and as Mrs. Jo liked odd penalties she tried it.

"All children run away," pleaded Nan, as if it were as natural and necessary a thing as measles or whooping cough.

"Not all, and some who do run away don't get found again," answered Mrs. Jo.

"Didn't you do it yourself?" asked Nan, whose keen little eyes saw some traces of a kindred spirit in the serious lady who was sewing so morally before her.

Mrs. Jo laughed, and owned that she did.

"Tell about it," demanded Nan, feeling that she was getting the upper hand in the discussion.

Mrs. Jo saw that, and sobered down at once, saying, with a remorseful shake of the head:

"I did it a good many times, and led my poor mother rather a hard life with my pranks, till she cured me."

"How?" and Nan sat up with a face full of interest.

"I had a new pair of shoes once, and wanted to show them; so, though I was told not to leave the garden, I ran away and was wandering about all day. It was in the city, and why I wasn't killed I don't know. Such a time as I had. I frolicked in the park with dogs, sailed boats in the Back Bay with strange boys, dined with a little Irish beggar girl on salt fish and potatoes, and was found at last fast asleep on a doorstep with my arms round a great dog. It was late in the evening, and I was as dirty as a little pig, and the new shoes were worn out—I had traveled so far."

"How nice!" cried Nan, looking all ready to go and do it herself.

"It was *not* nice next day," and Mrs. Jo tried to keep her eyes from betraying how much she enjoyed the memory of her early capers.

"Did your mother whip you?" asked Nan, curiously.

"She never whipped me but once, and then she begged my pardon, or I don't think I ever should have forgiven her, it hurt my feelings so much."

"Why did she beg your pardon?—my father doesn't."

"Because, when she had done it, I turned round and said, 'Well, you are mad yourself, and ought to be whipped as much as me.' She looked at me a minute, then her anger all died out, and she said, as if ashamed, 'You are right, Jo, I *am* angry; and why should I punish you for being in a passion when I set you such a bad example? Forgive me, dear, and let us try to help one another in a better way.' I never forgot it, and it did me more good than a dozen rods."

Nan sat thoughtfully turning the little cold-cream jar for a minute, and Mrs. Jo said nothing, but let that idea get well into the busy little mind that was so quick to see and feel what went on about her.

"I like that," said Nan, presently, and her face looked less elfish, with its sharp eyes, inquisitive nose, and mischievous mouth. "What did your mother do to you when you ran away that time?"

"She tied me up to the bedpost with a long string, so that I could not go out of the room, and there I stayed all day with the little worn-out shoes hanging up before me to remind me of my fault."

"I should think that *would* cure anybody," cried Nan, who loved her liberty above all things.

"It did cure me, and I think it will you, so I am going to try it," said Mrs. Jo, suddenly taking a ball of strong twine out of a drawer in her work table.

Nan looked as if she was decidedly getting the worst of the argument now, and sat feeling much crestfallen while Mrs. Jo tied one end round her waist and the other to the arm of the sofa, saying, as she finished:

"I don't like to tie you up like a naughty little dog, but if you don't remember any better than a dog, I must treat you like one."

"I'd just as lief be tied up as not—I like to play dog," and Nan put on a don't-care face, and began to growl and grovel on the floor.

Mrs. Jo took no notice, but leaving a book or two and a handkerchief to hem, she went away, and left Miss Nan to her own devices. This was not agreeable, and after sitting a moment she tried to untie the cord. But it was fastened in the belt of her apron behind, so she began on the knot at the other end. It soon came loose, and gathering it up, Nan was about to get out of the window, when she heard Mrs. Jo say to somebody as she passed through the hall:

"No, I don't think she will run away now; she is an honorable little girl, and knows that I do it to help her."

In a minute Nan whisked back, tied herself up, and began to sew violently. Rob came in a moment after, and was so charmed with the new punishment that he got a jump rope and tethered himself to the other arm of the sofa in the most social manner.

"I got lost too, so I ought to be tied up as much as Nan," he explained to his mother when she saw the new captive.

"I'm not sure that you don't deserve a little punishment, for you knew it was wrong to go far away from the rest."

"Nan took me," began Rob, willing to enjoy the novel penalty, but not willing to take the blame.

"You needn't have gone. You have a conscience, though you are a little boy, and you must learn to mind it."

"Well, my conscience didn't prick me a bit when she said, 'Let's get over the wall,' " answered Rob, quoting one of Demi's expressions.

"Did you stop to see if it did?"

"No."

"Then you cannot tell."

"I guess it's such a little conscience that it doesn't prick hard enough for me to feel it," added Rob, after thinking over the matter for a minute.

"We must sharpen it up. It's bad to have a dull conscience; so you may stay here till dinner time, and talk about it with Nan. I trust you both not to untie yourselves till I say the word."

"No, we won't," said both, feeling a certain sense of virtue in helping to punish themselves.

For an hour they were very good, then they grew tired of one room, and longed to get out. Never had the hall seemed so inviting; even the little bedroom acquired a sudden interest, and they would gladly have gone in and played tent with the curtains of the best bed. The open windows drove them wild because they could not reach them; and the outer world seemed so beautiful, they wondered how they ever found the heart to say it was dull. Nan pined for a race round the lawn, and Rob remembered with dismay that he had not fed his dog that morning, and wondered what poor Pollux would do. They watched the clock, and Nan did some nice calculations in minutes and seconds, while Rob learned to tell all the hours between eight and one so well that he never forgot them. It was maddening to smell the dinner, to know that there was to be succotash and huckleberry pudding, and to feel that they would not be on the spot to secure good helps of both. When Mary Ann began to set the table, they nearly cut themselves in two trying to see what meat there was to be; and Nan offered to help her make the beds, if she would only see that she had "lots of sauce on her pudding."

When the boys came bursting out of school, they found the children tugging at their halters like a pair of restive little colts, and were much edified, as well as amused, by the sequel to the exciting adventures of the night.

"Untie me now, Marmar; my conscience will prick like a pin next time, I know it will," said Rob, as the bell rang, and Teddy came to look at him with sorrowful surprise.

"We shall see," answered his mother, setting him free. He took a good run down the hall, back through the dining room, and brought up beside Nan, quite beaming with virtuous satisfaction.

"I'll bring her dinner to her, may I?" he asked, pitying his fellow captive.

"That's my kind little son! Yes, pull out the table, and get a chair," and Mrs. Jo hurried away to quell the ardor of the others, who were always in a raging state of hunger at noon.

Nan ate alone, and spent a long afternoon attached to the sofa. Mrs. Bhaer lengthened her bonds so that she could look out of the window; and there she stood watching the boys play, and all the little summer creatures enjoying their liberty. Daisy had a picnic for the dolls on the lawn, so that Nan might see the fun if she could not join in it. Tommy turned his best somersaults to console her; Demi sat on the steps reading aloud to himself, which amused Nan a good deal; and Dan brought a little tree toad to show her as the most delicate attention in his power.

But nothing atoned for the loss of freedom; and a few hours of confinement taught Nan how precious it was. A good many thoughts went through the little head that lay on the window sill during the last quiet hours when all the children went to the brook to see Emil's new ship launched. She was to have christened it, and had depended on smashing a tiny bottle of currant wine over the prow as it was named *Josephine* in honor of Mrs. Bhaer. Now she had lost her chance, and Daisy wouldn't do it half so well. Tears rose to her eyes as she remembered that it was all her own fault; and she said aloud, addressing a fat bee who was rolling about in the yellow heart of a rose just under the window:

"If you have run away, you'd better go right home, and tell your mother you are sorry, and never do so any more."

"I am glad to hear you give him such good advice, and I think he has taken it," said Mrs. Jo, smiling, as the bee spread his dusty wings and flew away.

Nan brushed off a bright drop or two that shone on the window sill, and nestled against her friend as she took her on her knee, adding kindly—for she had seen the little drops, and knew what they meant:

"Do you think my mother's cure for running away a good one?"

"Yes, ma'am," answered Nan, quite subdued by her quiet day.

"I hope I shall not have to try it again."

"I guess not," and Nan looked up with such an earnest little face that Mrs. Jo felt satisfied, and said no more, for she liked to have her penalties do their own work, and did not spoil the effect by too much moralizing.

Here Rob appeared, bearing with infinite care what Asia called a "sarcer pie," meaning one baked in a saucer.

"It's made out of some of my berries, and I'm going to give you half at supper time," he announced, with a flourish.

"What makes you, when I'm so naughty?" asked Nan, meekly.

"Because we got lost together. You aren't going to be naughty again, are you?"

"Never," said Nan, with great decision.

"Oh, goody! now let's go and get Mary Ann to cut this for us all ready to eat; it's 'most tea time," and Rob beckoned with the delicious little pie.

Nan started to follow, then stopped, and said:

"I forgot, I can't go."

"Try and see," said Mrs. Bhaer, who had quietly untied the cord sash while she had been talking.

Nan saw that she was free, and with one tempestuous kiss to Mrs. Jo, she was off like a humming bird, followed by Robby, dribbling huckleberry juice as he ran.

LIGHT VERSE

Mother Goose, the fictitious compiler of the revered collection of children's verses first published in 1791, was a name derived from a gathering of fairy tales by Charles Perrault, Contes de ma mère l'oye *(1697), which translates roughly as "old wives' tales."*

Robert Louis Stevenson (1850–1894), known especially for his adventure stories such as Treasure Island, *was also the author of a lighthearted collection of poetry entitled* A Child's Garden of Verses. *We offer a selection of favorites from each.*

FROM

Mother Goose's Nursery Rhymes

Sleep, Baby, Sleep

Sleep, baby, sleep,
Our cottage vale is deep;
The little lamb is on the green,
With woolly fleece so soft
 and clean—
  Sleep, baby, sleep!

Sleep, baby, sleep,
Down where the woodbines creep;
Be always like the lamb so mild,
A kind, and sweet, and gentle
 child—
  Sleep, baby, sleep!

Hush-a-Bye, Baby

Hush-a-bye, baby,
On the tree top,

When the wind blows,
The cradle will rock;

When the bough breaks,
The cradle will fall,

Down tumbles baby,
Cradle, and all.

Dance, Little Baby

Dance, little Baby, dance up high,
Never mind, Baby, Mother is by;
Crow and caper, caper and crow,
There, little Baby, there you go;
Up to the ceiling, down to the ground,
Backwards and forwards, round and round;
Dance, little Baby, and Mother will sing,
With the merry coral, ding, ding, ding!

What Are Little Boys Made Of?

What are little boys made of, made of?
What are little boys made of?
Snips and snails, and puppy-dogs' tails;
That's what little boys are made of, made of.

What are little girls made of, made of?
What are little girls made of?
Sugar and spice, and all things nice,
That's what little girls are made of, made of.

The Old Woman Who Lived in a Shoe

There was an old woman who lived in a shoe,

She had so many children she didn't know what to do;

She gave them some broth without any bread,

Then whipped them all round, and sent them to bed.

Monday's Child

Monday's child is fair of face,
Tuesday's child is full of grace,
Wednesday's child is full of woe,
Thursday's child has far to go,
Friday's child is loving and giving,
Saturday's child works hard for its living,
But the child that is born on the Sabbath day
Is bonny, and blithe, and good, and gay.

Baby Bunting

Baby, baby bunting,
Father's gone a-hunting,

Mother's gone a-milking,
Sister's gone a-silking,

Brother's gone to buy a skin
To wrap the baby bunting in.

The Three Kittens

Three little kittens lost their mittens,
And they began to cry,
"Oh, Mother dear,
We very much fear
That we have lost our mittens!"

"Lost your mittens!
You naughty kittens!
Then you shall have no pie.
Mee-ow, mee-ow, mee-ow!
No, you shall have no pie.
Mee-ow, mee-ow, mee-ow!"

The three little kittens found their mittens,
And they began to cry,
"Oh, Mother dear,
See here, see here,
See, we have found our mittens!"

"Put on your mittens,
You silly kittens,
And you shall have some pie.
Purr-r, purr-r, purr-r!"
"Oh, let us have the pie!
Purr-r, purr-r, purr-r!"

The three little kittens put on their mittens,
   And soon ate up the pie;
      "Oh, Mother dear,
      We greatly fear
That we have soiled our mittens!"

   "Soiled your mittens!
   You naughty kittens!"
Then they began to sigh,
   Mi-ow, mi-ow, mi-ow!
Then they began to sigh,
   Mi-ow, mi-ow, mi-ow!

The three little kittens washed their mittens,
   And hung them up to dry;
      "Oh, Mother dear,
      Do you not hear
That we have washed our mittens!"

   "Washed your mittens!
   Oh, you're good kittens!
But I smell a rat close by.
   Hush! hush! mee-ow, mee-ow."
"We smell a rat close by,
   Mee-ow, mee-ow, mee-ow!"

Rock-a-by, Baby

Rock-a-by, baby, thy cradle is green;
Father's a nobleman, mother's a queen;
And Betty's a lady, and wears a gold ring;
And Johnny's a drummer, and drums for the king.

FROM

A Child's Garden of Verses

Robert Louis Stevenson

To Alison Cunningham from Her Boy

For the long nights you lay awake
And watched for my unworthy sake:
For your most comfortable hand
That led me through the uneven land:
For all the story-books you read,
For all the pains you comforted,
For all you pitied, all you bore,
In sad and happy days of yore:—
My second mother, my first wife,
The angel of my infant life—
From the sick child, now well and old,
Take, nurse, the little book you hold!

And grant it, heaven, that all who read
May find as dear a nurse at need,
And every child who lists my rhyme,
In the bright fireside, nursery clime,
May hear it in as kind a voice
As made my childish days rejoice!

The Land of Storybooks

At evening when the lamp is lit,
Around the fire my parents sit;
They sit at home and talk and sing,
And do not play at anything.

Now, with my little gun, I crawl
All in the dark along the wall,
And follow round the forest track
Away behind the sofa back.

There, in the night, where none can spy,
All in my hunter's camp I lie,
And play at books that I have read
Till it is time to go to bed.

These are the hills, there are the woods,
These are my starry solitudes;
And there the river by whose brink
The roaring lions come to drink.

I see the others far away
As if in firelit camp they lay,
And I, like to an Indian scout,
Around their party prowled about.

So, when my nurse comes in for me,
Home I return across the sea,
And go to bed with backward looks
At my dear land of Storybooks.

Young Night Thought

All night long, and every night
When my mamma puts out the light,
I see the people marching by,
As plain as day, before my eye.

Armies and emperors and kings,
All carrying different kinds of things,
And marching in so grand a way,
You never saw the like by day.

So fine a show was never seen
At the great circus on the green;
For every kind of beast and man
Is marching in that caravan.

At first they move a little slow,
But still the faster on they go.
And still beside them close I keep
Until we reach the town of Sleep.

Whole Duty of Children

A child should always say what's true
And speak when he is spoken to,
And behave mannerly at table:
At least as far as he is able.

The Sun's Travels

The sun is not a-bed when I
At night upon my pillow lie;
Still round the earth his way he takes,
And morning after morning makes.

While here at home, in shining day,
We round the sunny garden play,
Each little Indian sleepy-head
Is being kissed and put to bed.

And when at eve I rise from tea,
Day dawns beyond the Atlantic Sea,
And all the children in the West
Are getting up and being dressed.

Northwest Passage

1. GOOD NIGHT

When the bright lamp is carried in,
The sunless hours again begin;
O'er all without, in field and lane,
The haunted night returns again.

Now we behold the embers flee
About the firelit hearth; and see
Our faces painted as we pass,
Like pictures, on the window-glass.

Must we to bed indeed? Well then,
Let us arise and go like men,
And face with an undaunted tread
The long black passage up to bed.

Farewell, O brother, sister, sire!
O pleasant party round the fire!
The songs you sing, the tales you tell,
Till far to-morrow, fare ye well!

2. SHADOW MARCH

All round the house is the jet-black night;
   It stares through the window-pane;
It crawls in the corners, hiding from the light,
   And it moves with the moving flame.

Now my little heart goes a-beating like a drum,
   With the breath of the Bogie in my hair;
And all round the candle the crooked shadows come
   And go marching along up the stair.

The shadow of the balusters, the shadow of the lamp,
   The shadow of the child that goes to bed—
All the wicked shadows coming, tramp, tramp, tramp,
   With the black night overhead.

3. IN PORT

Last, to the chamber where I lie
My fearful footsteps patter nigh,
And come from out the cold and gloom
Into my warm and cheerful room.

There, safe arrived, we turn about
To keep the coming shadows out,
And close the happy door at last
On the perils that we past.

Then, when mamma goes by to bed,
She shall come in with tip-toe tread,
And see me lying warm and fast
And in the Land of Nod at last.

To Willie and Henrietta

If two may read aright
These rhymes of old delight
And house and garden play,
You two, my cousins, and you only, may.

You in a garden green
With me were king and queen,
Were hunter, soldier, tar,
And all the thousand things that children are.

Now in the elders' seat
We rest with quiet feet,
And from the window-bay
We watch the children, our successors, play.

'Time was,' the golden head
Irrevocably said;
But time which none can bind,
While flowing fast away, leaves love behind.

To My Mother

You too, my mother, read my rhymes
For love of unforgotten times
And you may chance to hear once more
The little feet along the floor.

To Minnie

The red room with the giant bed
Where none but elders laid their head;
The little room where you and I
Did for awhile together lie
And, simple suitor, I you hand
In decent marriage did demand;
The great day nursery, best of all,
With pictures pasted on the wall
And leaves upon the blind—
A pleasant room wherein to wake
And hear the leafy garden shake
And rustle in the wind—
And pleasant there to lie in bed
And see the pictures overhead—
The wars about Sebastopol,
The grinning guns along the wall,
The daring escalade,
The plunging ships, the bleating sheep,
The happy children ankle-deep
And laughing as they wade;

All these are vanished clean away,
And the old manse is changed to-day;
It wears an altered face
And shields a stranger race.
The river, on from mill to mill,
Flows past our childhood's garden still;
But ah! we children never more
Shall watch it from the water-door!
Below the yew—it still is there—
Our phantom voices haunt the air
As we were still at play,
And I can hear them call and say:
'*How far is it to Babylon?*'

Ah, far enough, my dear,
Far, far enough from here—
Yet you have farther gone.!
'*Can I get there by candlelight?*'
So goes the old refrain.
I do not know—perchance you might—
But only, children, hear it right,
Ah, never to return again!
The eternal dawn, beyond a doubt,
Shall break on hill and plain,
And put all stars and candles out,
Ere we be young again.

To you in distant India, these
I send across the seas,
Nor count it far across.
For which of us forgets

The Indian cabinets,
The bones of antelope, the wings of albatross.
The pied and painted birds and beans,
The junks and bangles, beads and screens,
The gods and sacred bells,
And the loud-humming, twisted shells?
The level of the parlour floor
Was honest, homely, Scottish shore;
But when we climbed upon a chair,
Behold the gorgeous East was there!
Be this a fable; and behold
Me in the parlour as of old,
And Minie just above me set
In the quaint Indian cabinet!
Smiling and kind, you grace a shelf
Too high for me to reach myself.
Reach down a hand, my dear, and take
These rhymes for old acquaintance' sake.

To My Name-Child

1

Some day soon this rhyming volume, if you learn with proper speed,
Little Louis Sanchez, will be given you to read.
Then shall you discover, that your name was printed down
By the English printers, long before, in London town.

In the great and busy city where the East and West are met,
All the little letters did the English printer set;
While you thought of nothing, and were still too young to play,
Foreign people thought of you in places far away.

Ay, and while you slept, a baby, over all the English lands
Other little children took the volume in their hands;
Other children questioned, in their homes across the seas:
Who was Little Louis, won't you tell us, mother, please?

2

Now that you have spelt your lesson, lay it down and go and play,
Seeking shells and seaweed on the sands of Monterey,
Watching all the mighty whalebones, lying buried by the breeze,
Tiny sandy-pipers, and the huge Pacific seas.

And remember in your playing, as the sea-fog rolls to you,
Long ere you could read it, how I told you what to do;
And that while you thought of no one, nearly half the world away
Some one thought of Louis on the beach of Monterey!

The Land of Nod

From breakfast on through all the day
At home among friends I stay,
But every night I go abroad
Afar into the land of Nod.

All by myself I have to go,
With none to tell me what to do—
All alone beside the streams
And up the mountainsides of dreams.

The strangest things are there for me,
Both things to eat and things to see,
And many frightening sights abroad
Till morning in the land of Nod.

Try as I like to find the way,
I never can get back by day,
Nor can remember plain and clear
The curious music that I hear.

To Any Reader

As from the house your mother sees
You playing round the garden trees,
So you may see, if you will look
Through the windows of this book,
Another child, far, far away,
And in another garden, play.
But do not think you can at all,
By knocking on the window, call
That child to hear you. He intent
Is all on his play-business bent.
He does not hear; he will not look,
Nor yet be lured out of his book.
For, long ago, the truth to say,
He has grown up and gone away,
And it is but a child of air
That lingers in the garden there.

FROM MEDITATIONS DIVINE AND MORAL

BY ANNE BRADSTREET

Anne Bradstreet (c. 1612–1672) was among the best known of Puritan-era American poets and was the first recognized female poet of her era. In 1664, she wrote a collection of truisms for her son Simon, to which she appended this dedicatory letter: "Parents perpetuate their lives in their posterity and their manners; in their imitation children do naturally rather follow the failings than the virtues of their predecessors, but I am persuaded better things of you. You once desired me to leave something for you in writing that you might look upon, when you should see me no more; I could think of nothing more fit for you nor of more ease to myself than these short meditations following. Such as they are, I bequeath to you; small legacies are accepted by true friends, much more by dutiful children. I have avoided encroaching upon others' conceptions because I would leave you nothing but mine own, though in value they fall short of all in this kind; yet I presume they will be better prized by you for the author's sake. The Lord bless you with grace here and crown you with glory hereafter, that I may meet you with rejoicing at that great day of appearing, which is the continual prayer of your affectionate mother, A.B."

1

There is no object that we see, no action that we do, no good that we enjoy, no evil that we feel or fear, but we may make some spiritual advantage of all; and he that makes such improvement is wise as well as pious.

2

Many can speak well, but few can do well. We are better scholars in the theory than the practic part, but he is a true Christian that is a proficient in both.

4

A ship that bears much sail and little or no ballast is easily overset, and that man whose head hath great abilities and his heart little or no grace is in danger of foundering.

9

Sweet words are like honey: a little may refresh, but too much gluts the stomach.

10

Diverse children have their different natures: some are like flesh which nothing but salt will keep from putrefaction, some again like tender fruits that are best preserved with sugar. Those parents are wise that can fit their nurture according to their nature.

12

Authority without wisdom is like a heavy axe without an edge: fitter to bruise than polish.

13

The reason why Christians are so loath to exchange this world for a better is because they have more sense than faith: they see what they enjoy; they do but hope for that which is to come.

15

A low man can go upright under that door where a taller is glad to stoop; so a man of weak faith and mean abilities may undergo a cross more patiently than he that excels him both in gifts and graces.

16

That house which is not often swept makes the cleanly inhabitant soon loath it, and that heart which is not continually purifying itself is no fit temple for the spirit of God to dwell in.

18

He that will undertake to climb up a steep mountain with a great burden on his back will find it a wearisome if not an impossible task; so he that thinks to mount to heaven clogged with the cares and riches of this life, 'tis no wonder if he faint by the way.

19

Corn, till it have past through the mill and been ground to powder, is not fit for bread. God so deals with his servants: he grinds them with grief and pain till they turn to dust, and then are they fit manchet for his mansion.

32

Ambitious men are like hops that never rest climbing so long as they have anything to stay upon, but take away their props, and they are of all the most dejected.

33

Much labour wearies the body, and many thoughts oppress the mind; man aims at profit by the one and content in the other, but often misses of both and finds nothing but vanity and vexation of spirit.

34

Dim eyes are the concomitants of old age, and shortsightedness in those that are eyes of a republic fortells a declining state.

35

We read in Scriptures of three sorts of arrows: the arrow of an enemy, the arrow of pestilence, and the arrow of a slanderous tongue. The two first kill the body, the last the good name; the two former leave a man when he is once dead, but the last mangles him in his grave.

36

Sore labourers have hard hands and old sinners have brawny consciences.

40

The spring is a lively emblem of the resurrection: after a long winter we see the leafless trees and dry stocks (at the approach of the sun) to resume their former vigor and beauty in a more ample manner than what they lost in the autumn; so shall it be at that great day after a long vacation, when the Sun of righteousness shall appear; those dry bones shall arise in far more glory than that which they lost at their creation, and in this transcends the spring that their leaf shall never fail nor their sap decline.

43

Fire hath its force abated by water, not by wind, and anger must be allayed by cold words and not by blustering threats.

47

A shadow in the parching sun and a shelter in a blustering storm are of all seasons the most welcome; so a faithful friend in time of adversity is of all other most comfortable.

48

There is nothing admits of more admiration than God's various dispensation of His gifts among the songs of men, betwixt whom He hath put so vast a disproportion that they scarcely seem made of the same lump or sprung out of the loins of one Adam, some set in the highest dignity that mortality is capable of, and some again so base that they are viler than the earth, some so wise and learned that they seem like angels among men, and some again so ignorant and sottish that they are more like beasts than men, some pious saints, some incarnate devils, some exceeding beautiful, and some extremely deformed, some so strong and healthful that their bones are full of marrow and their breast of milk, and some again so weak and feeble that while they live they are accounted among the dead; and no other reason can be given of all this but so it pleased Him whose will is the perfect rule of righteousness.

49

The treasures of this world may well be compared to husks, for they have no kernal in them, and they that feed upon them may soon stuff their throats, but cannot fill their bellies. They may be choked by them, but cannot be satisfied with them.

50

Sometimes the sun is only shadowed by a cloud that we cannot see his luster although we may walk by his light, but when he is set, we are in darkness till he arise again. So God doth sometime veil His face but for a moment that we cannot behold the light of His countenance as at some other time, yet He affords so much light as may direct our way, that we may go forwards to the city of habitation, but when He seems to set and be quite gone out of sight, then must we needs walk in darkness and see no light; yet then must we trust in the Lord and stay upon our God, and when the morning (which is the appointed time) is come, the Sun of righteousness will arise with healing in His wings.

55

We read of ten lepers that were cleansed but of one that returned thanks; we are more ready to receive mercies than we are to acknowledge them. Men can use great importunity when they are in distresses and show great ingratitude after their successes, but he that ordereth his conversation aright will glorify him that heard him in the day of his trouble.

67

All the works and doings of God are wonderful, but none more awful than His great work of election and reprobation; when we consider how many good parents have had bad children, and again how many bad parents have had pious children, it should make us adore the sovereignty of God, who will not be tied to time nor place, nor yet to persons, but takes and chooses, when and where and whom He pleases; it should also teach the children of godly parents to walk with fear and trembling, lest they through unbelief fall short of a promise; it may also be a support to such as have or had wicked parents, that if they abide not in unbelief, God is able to gaff them in. The upshot of all should make us with the apostle to admire the justice and mercy of God and say how unsearchable are His ways and His footsteps past finding out.

72

As the brands of a fire, if once severed, will of themselves go out although you use no other means to extinguish them, so distance of place together with length of time (if there be no intercourse) will cool the affections of intimate friends, though there should be no displeasance between them.

74

Well doth the apostle call riches "deceitful" riches, and they may truly be compared to deceitful friends who speak fair and promise much but perform nothing, and so leave those in the lurch that most relied on them; so is it with the wealth, honours, and pleasures of this world which miserably delude men and make them put great confidence in them, but when death threatens and distress lays hold upon them, they prove like the reeds of Egypt that pierce instead of supporting, like empty wells in the time of drought that those that go to find water in them return with their empty pitchers ashamed.

A Note on the Type

The principal text of this Modern Library edition
was set in a digitized version of Janson,
a typeface that dates from about 1690 and was cut by Nicholas Kis,
a Hungarian working in Amsterdam. The original matrices have
survived and are held by the Stempel foundry in Germany.
Hermann Zapf redesigned some of the weights and sizes for Stempel, basing his revisions on the original design.

A Note on the Type

The principal text of this Modern Library edition was set in a digitized version of Janson, a typeface that dates from about 1690 and was cut by Nicholas Kis, a Hungarian working in Amsterdam. The original matrices have survived and are held by the Stempel foundry in Germany. Hermann Zapf redesigned some of the weights and sizes for Stempel, basing his revisions on the original design.